The Dark Side of the Moon

- ELIZABETH CARTY -

An environmentally friendly book printed and bound in England by
www.printondemand-worldwide.com

www.fast-print.net/store.php

The Dark Side of the Moon
Copyright © Elizabeth Carty 2011

ISBN 978-184426-988-4

First published 2011 by
FASTPRINT PUBLISHING
Peterborough, England.

Elizabeth Carty is a native of Loch Gowna, County Cavan. She has been living and working in County Meath for the past 25 years.

Her short stories have won several national and international awards. She is three times winner of the George Birmingham Short Story Prize. *The Dark Side of the Moon* was short listed for the U.K Writer of the Year Award in 2008. She has been a contributor to RTE's *A Living Word, Sunday Miscellany,* and Lyric FM's *A Quiet Quarter.* Her stories have been short-listed for the Francis McManus Awards on several occasions and her work has been published in a number of anthologies.

Elizabeth is chairperson of the Irish Writers Union and has served on the executive committee of the Union since 2008. She is also a member of the Board of the Irish Copyright Licensing Agency. She works as a part–time Creative Writing Facilitator for County Meath V.E.C. and is currently completing her first novel, *'When The Mockingbird Sings'.*

House Private was short-listed for the Francis Mc. Manus Awards 2004 and has since been broadcast by RTE Radio One. *Dancing in the Snow* won the AIB/Ballina Festival Award in 2002. It was first published in *Ireland's Own. June Roses* was short listed for the Bill Naughton Literary Award in 1996. It was awarded second prize in the South Tipperary Arts Centre Awards in 1999. *The Listeners* was awarded second prize in the R.P Ireland Short Story Competition in 1996 and won the George A Birmingham Award in 2002 and the Drogheda Creative Awards in 2004. It was short-listed for Francis McManus Awards 2003. *Watchman, What of the Night?* was short-listed for the Francis McManus Award 2009. *I Believe in Angels* was a prize winner in the 2001 Maria Edgeworth Short Story Competition. *Daisy Chains* was the winner of the Nora Fahy Literary Award in 1997. *Burnt Umber* was short listed for the Sword Heritage festival award 2003. *I Am The Song –Sing Me* won second prize in the 2001 Francis McManus Short Story Competition. *Cat's Eyes* won the Drogheda Lifestyle Short Story Award in 1999. *The Dark Side of the Moon* won The Luas Literary Award 2001, second prize in the Irish News International Short Story Award 2000, The George A. Birmingham Award 2001, second prize in South Tipperary Arts Festival Award 2001 and the Feile Iorras Award 2001. *Disco Queen* was the 1998 winner of Bookwise Award. *For Better or Worse* was a prize winner in the AIB /Ballina Festival, the Cootehill Arts Festival 2002 and the Maria Edgeworth Short Story Competition 2003. *The Sound of Many Waters* was awarded third prize in the Nora Fahy Awards 1998. *Lighting the Star* was short-listed for the Bill Naughton Short Story award 1996 and was broadcast on Lyric FM. *The Butterfly Jug* was the winner of the Bill Naughton

Short Story Award. *Nancy* was short-listed for the Spotlight on Skerries Award 1998 Awards and the Irish News International Awards 1999. *The War Isn't Over Yet* was awarded first prize in the Ballina Arts Festival 1997. *Whistling in the Dark* was short listed in the Fish Awards of 1998.

This book is dedicated to the memory of my
brother Padraic.

Contents

Acknowledgements.

Acknowledgements are due to the editors of the following publications and broadcasters in which some of the short stories in this collection first appeared; Ireland's Own, The Meath Chronicle, RTE, Splinters 1 Anthology, The Edgeworth Papers, Volume VI Anthology, Departures 1 1997, The Edgeworth Papers, Vol. VII 2003, Departures 2 1998, and Splinters 2 Anthology.

I wish also to acknowledge the support of Cavan County Council Arts Awards, with the assistance of the Arts Council, who facilitated the publication of this anthology.

My grateful thanks to Liam Mac Uistin, distinguished author, playwright, and poet, whose words of encouragement first prompted the publication of this collection.

To my family, Eleanora and Francie, and especially to Rita who was always there to support me, win, lose or draw. Thank you for everything.

To my late mother, Katie, a wonderful story teller who taught me the true meaning of courage.

Finally, love and thanks to my daughters, Niamh and Aisling, for your tireless proof- reading and constant encouragement and support.

And to Noel - thank you for believing in me. I couldn't have done any of it without you.

Foreword

For many generations Irish writers, from Moore to O'Connor, O Faoláin, McGahern and many others have embellished the art of the short story with their own special flair and power.

This collection of short stories by Elizabeth Carty is no exception. It takes a deep, emotional, and humorous look at the Ireland of today, and at the way its people have evolved with the changing times.

It is especially remarkable for the colour and power of its language. The collection portrays, in compelling and powerful words, gripping pictures of young and old in a modern, changing Ireland. These striking and authentic portrayals are presented with a wit and a verve that makes this collection truly a lasting pleasure to enjoy.

LIAM MAC UISTIN.

JUNE ROSES

Jack was a bit odd, according to his neighbours. A decent man and a good Christian but odd all the same. The youngest of nine children, and a confirmed bachelor, he had lived alone since his parents died. His brothers and sisters had gone away. One brother to New Zealand, two sisters to Canada, the rest to New York. They had married and made new lives for themselves in their adopted countries. Most of them hadn't been home in years.

His parents had lived to a respectable old age. His father died first, his mother fifteen years later. Shortly after her death the more outspoken of his female neighbours had suggested that he should find a wife 'to look after him.' Jack had pushed his flat cap to the back of his head with his big, raw-knuckled hand and stared at her steadily from cool, grey eyes.

'*I'm thankful to you for bothering your head about me,*' was all he said.

'*The old fool,*' the woman blustered to her husband later. '*Who'd be bothered with him anyway? I'd like to see him trying to romance a woman.*'

Jack's house was small, neat, picturesque, tucked tidily into the side of a hill half a mile up a narrow lane. He whitewashed the walls every Easter time because his father had done it before him and repainted the door and window ledges a deep, sombre blue.

The house was beautiful in summer, bordered by meadows lush with buttercups and ragged robin and great smiling daisies with golden, unwinking eyes. On bright

1

mornings the sun came tumbling down the hill and played hide and seek among the tall grasses of the uncut meadows. Winter swept the fields bare of their beauty and they huddled sullenly under their comfortless covering of frost. Jack never noticed either way. They were just the road fields and he rented them out to a neighbour.

Summer tourists sometimes stopped at the road gate, drawn by the sight of an elusive wisp of smoke and the gleam of whitewashed gable as their rented cars swept down the hill from the town. Jack welcomed the tourists with morose courtesy, bewildered at their exclamations of delighted admiration for the house and the flower-filled meadows. He'd consent with shy reluctance to have his photograph taken and stood stiff and ill-at-ease against the backdrop of rough whitewashed walls and the pink, blowsy roses that, like the house, had been a part of his life for as long as he could remember. Sometimes, in an idle moment, he pulled away some dead leaves or cut back a too-vigorous shoot that was smothering the light from the windows. The roses shook out their pale skirts, drenching the summer air with sweetness, and went on growing.

Months later, in Birmingham or New York or Sydney, the tourists, from the comfort of their air-conditioned, centrally heated offices would sigh wistfully as they passed around their holiday pictures to bored friends and colleagues, marvelling anew at the tranquillity and beauty of the little house and the charming eccentricity of its owner.

'*That old fellow,*' they'd say, '*he doesn't know how lucky he is.*'

But by the time summer came around again they would have forgotten all about him.

Jack, if he thought about it at all, thought that the house was damp and cold, even in summer, and too far away from the town. His neighbours were kind and well-meaning but his was not the nature to invite friendship. He accepted their presence in his life as he did the house and the meadows that surrounded it and the narrow stony lane, a part of the life he had always known. The younger people of the townland, home on holidays from England, would sometimes drive up the laneway, driven by boredom and bad weather and the desire to show off their pretty wives and noisy, fractious children.

'Wait until you meet Jack,' they told their wives, *'he's as odd as two left feet.'*

Jack welcomed his visitors with the same calm politeness with which he greeted the summer tourists. He poured tea or carefully hoarded whiskey as he listened to their talk of Princess Street or Cricklewood or Luton – places that were as alien to him as Mars. He gave the children money, offering the silver coins gravely and the children accepted his gifts with the same, unsmiling gravity, a transaction among equals.

The young wives sat on uncomfortable chairs in the dim kitchen and silently coveted the worn dresser and faded delph that their own mothers had long since discarded in favour of brightly coloured laminate and plastic. Gazing covetously at the dull golds and blues of the five big platters that marched along the top of the dresser and the smoke-dulled grandfather clock that ticked away stolidly in a darkened corner, they wondered if they might offer to buy them from Jack, but lost courage in the face of his calm, taciturn courtesy. If they'd asked him, Jack would have given the things away for nothing. He placed no value on them, the clock was old and cumbersome and a poor time-keeper and the plates had never been used, not even in his mother's time. They were less use to him than the ugly, functional mugs that he kept on a long shelf over the fireplace.

Everything in the house was functional except for the plastic bottle full of Knock holy water that stood on one deep windowsill beside a fat brown jug and two virulent, yellow vases, their surfaces chipped and pitted, that had once belonged to his mother. The jug had a broken spout. Jack used it to hold rusted nails and holy medals and odd bits of string.

He treated women with quiet, courteous diffidence. Those who were married he referred to as 'so-and so's woman.' He didn't intend such remarks to be offensive or disrespectful to his female neighbours. They were, as his own mother had been, a necessary part of the order of things, an extension of their husband's lives.

When he spoke of his mother, which was seldom, he mentioned her as casually as if he was discussing the weather or the rearing of the hay, with no discernable fondness or even emotion in his voice.

In the first week of June each year he washed the vases carefully and filled them with carelessly arranged handfuls of roses. He placed them on the window ledge in the kitchen where they sat until they withered away, incongruous among the old letters and calendars and his Sunday cap. It was a thing to be wondered at among his neighbours and some said that his mother had done the same thing-every June she had set the vases on the window ledge and filled them with roses. Nobody ever asked Jack if the story was true but when she died twenty years earlier he'd brought her body home from the hospital to be waked and laid her coffin between two chairs in the kitchen and placed the two yellow vases, filled with roses, on the floor on either side. It was late August, and the flowers looked bedraggled and faded, dropping their petals in untidy profusion on the newly swept floor. A well-meaning neighbour had moved them, suggesting that they might look tidier on the dresser. He had nodded silently and the woman bustled away, satisfied. Later she noticed that they had been replaced beside the coffin and had turned away, her face reddening, feeling resentful and ashamed.

They waked his mother for two nights. Jack sat at the head of the coffin, composed and morose as always, a brown rosary slipping ceaselessly through his fingers, seemingly oblivious to the gentle murmur of gossip and prayers that surrounded him. Nobody tried to offer comfort, beyond the usual self-conscious handshake and mumbled *'sorry for your troubles.'*

Before the coffin was finally closed, after the last prayers were said, the priest touched him gently on the shoulder and he stood and looked into his mother's face and traced a cross on her cold forehead with his thumb. When he turned away his face was calm. A few of the woman wept quietly as the coffin was finally raised on neighbour's shoulders and carried down the narrow lane to the waiting hearse. Jack closed the door behind the last of the mourners and followed, walking among his neighbours.

Some months afterwards he began going to the town on Sunday nights, walking the four miles there and back. He drank alone, sitting on a barstool at the corner of the grocery counter. He never offered to buy a drink for anyone, nor accepted any in return but sometimes a young man, a returned emigrant, or a near neighbour, would find an unexpected glass in front of him and Jack, raising a hand in acknowledgment and half-hearted farewell, already leaving. Once the publican had asked him about this odd practice. Jack only said, *'weren't we all young one time.'* and turned back morosely to his drink. The publican, a young man still in his thirties, didn't broach the subject again.

A brother in America wrote sporadically. He'd gone away as a young man and had only been home once, just after their mother died. The others never wrote except at Christmas, long letters with dollar bills folded between the sheets of flimsy airmail paper. Jack read the letters and put them behind the clock on the window ledge and forgot all about them. He put the money in the envelope and gave it to the woman who owned the local shop. He didn't like banks. A few days later she'd hand the envelope back and he'd fold the notes carefully away, uncounted, in the back of his purse.

He was taken ill suddenly at Sunday Mass. People said that it was a blessing that it should have happened like this, with help close at hand. He might have been lying on the kitchen floor for a week they said, helpless and people not knowing.

For weeks he lay motionless in the narrow hospital bed, his right side paralysed and his face twisted into a grotesque parody of a smile. The woman from the shop visited regularly, bringing him books he couldn't read, fruit he couldn't eat. They both knew that he was dying. He tried to tell her that he wanted to be brought home to be waked in his own house. Like his mother, he said, his voice horribly distorted. The woman touched his hand and nodded her understanding. The neighbours would look after their own. In a minute he was asleep and she fancied she saw peace on the tired, twisted face.

He died in the third week of June, slipping away quietly in his sleep in the dead hours before dawn. His body was taken home and placed in the bed in the small room beyond the kitchen where he had slept, a room none of them had ever seen. The women made tea and piled sandwiches and apple tarts on bright plastic plates and the blue and gold platters remained undisturbed on their high, dusty shelf.

When the last prayers were being said and the coffin finally closed, some of the young men were amazed and ashamed to find their eyes filling with tears. They shook their heads impatiently like angry bulls, avoiding each other's eyes, and went to town and got drunk.

Jack's nearest neighbours carried the coffin down the lane between drifts of meadowsweet and dog roses. They spoke of the dead man and those who had gone before him, but their talk was mostly of their own affairs, how the grass was nearly ready for cutting, and how the young ones would soon be home from Dublin or England for the holidays. A blackbird called to its mate and was answered, the soft notes rising and falling again to silence on the still air. Someone said, sighing, *'poor Jack will be missed'* and there was a nod of agreement from those around him.

The woman from the shop was the last to leave the house. She rearranged the chairs neatly along the walls and closed the door firmly on the silence and pulled a handful of buds from the rosebush as she passed. She hurried down the lane and reached the road gate, half breathless. As the coffin was slid into the hearse she threw the flowers on its smooth, shining surface. They slid across the lid and came to rest against the garish crucifix, gleaming cruelly in the late evening sun.

The hearse moved slowly up the hill and past the crossroads and round by the river field. The flowers mirrored in shining glass reflected back on themselves endlessly. To people waiting at intervals along the road to join the cortege it looked as if the coffin was surrounded by roses.

HOUSE PRIVATE

Bridgie stood in the middle of the dim, crowded kitchen, wiping an already clean dish absentmindedly with the corner of her apron. A folding table with rickety legs slouched carelessly against the wall behind her, surrounded by cardboard boxes that were filled with jugs, spare mugs, linen cloths, china tea sets-the trappings of hospitality that went from house to house during wakes, weddings, and visits from returned emigrants, missionary priests, American relations.

Eamonn, her son, sitting in his father's chair, pushed tinned salmon round his plate with moody resignation and then pushed the plate away and lit a cigarette.

'You can't stay here alone, it's far too isolated.' He smiled patiently at his mother as he ticked off the house's deficiencies on smooth, manicured fingers.

'You have no phone, no car. There's no proper damp course, no bathroom, no central heating. It would cost a fortune to make the place liveable; we could build a granny flat for half the money. The boys will love having you, we all will.'

Bridgie's grandsons, eating greedily, acknowledged their father's comments with monosyllabic, teenage contempt.

'Claudia agrees with me-don't you darling?' Eamonn turned towards his pale, elegant wife.

Claudia nodded silently, cutting Bridgie's brown bread into thin slivers, nibbling around the edges as delicately as a cat.

Bridgie wiped a saucer and placed it absentmindedly on the dresser.

'This house reared three generations. It'll last me out my time. I have good neighbours, the chapel beside me and the shed full of turf against the winter.'

She sighed.

'But it'll be a quiet house without your father-a quiet house.'

After they'd gone she sat, waiting for the house to settle itself again into the silence. In these three dim rooms, the little fields beyond, she knew the shape of every bush, the fall of every friendly shadow. Everything was in its familiar place-the Sacred Heart picture over the window, the nail on the back door for Ned's coat, the clock that hadn't ticked for twenty years. She thought of Ned, coming in from the milking, carrying a bucket in chapped and reddened hands, lying on a white counterpane in the room where they had slept all of their married life, his fingers awkwardly entwined on the starched, linen sheet, knotted and knurled like the roots of an old tree only half hidden by the clay - pale and beautiful in death.

When she twisted her ankle coming from Mass, the postman, on red alert since Ned died, phoned Eamonn in Dublin.

She left the house as it was - mugs on the dresser, the turf box full of turf, the buckets for feeding the calves outside the back door. She took with her the statue of the Child of Prague and her pictures; the Sacred Heart, De Valera, The Little Flower, John F. Kennedy and his wife Jacqueline wearing a pearl necklace, her dark hair glossy as a blackbird's wing. Outside the henhouse the red rambling rose that Ned's mother had planted was in bloom, galloping exuberantly across the gable end of the house, over the byre wall.

She gave Ned's dog to a neighbour.

'*Goodbye now, Whiskey,*' she said, '*good dog, good dog.*'

Her voice glutinous with buried sadness.

She sat on the bus, her shopping bag with the last of the duck eggs, her prayer book and rosary beads, a bottle of Lourdes holy water, two rounds of soda-bread, held tightly on her lap. A young girl in tight, faded jeans sat opposite, beating time with one slender hand to music only she could hear. Bridgie turned away, watched the Ballinagh road disappear into the distance with tearless, unseeing eyes.

Claudia met her at Store Street. Eamonn was in Brussels he wouldn't be home until Monday.

She was dumbfounded by the vividness of Claudia's kitchen. Chrome stools standing sentinel against ochre - painted walls. A dresser full of blue and white china. A straw hat, trimmed with dried flowers, tossed artlessly on a rocking chair. On the walls a set of prints of unlikely looking farm animals: cows, a cockerel, a sheep with a thin, supercilious smile.

They ate outside on a patio that was covered in pale yellow gravel the colour of scattered oats. Bridgie, seated stoically on a narrow, wrought–iron chair tasted, without recognition; basil, tagliatelli, oregano, sun–dried tomatoes, the pungent bite of garlic. The thin tracery of varicose veins on Claudia's long, tanned legs looked like maps drawn in faded ink. On the wall behind her a stone-cheeked cherub dribbled like a teething baby, bright droplets of water falling one by one, down his rounded pitted chin.

The granny flat smelled of paint and freshly sawn wood. Everything was new, unfaded: the sheer curtains at the window, the vase of pure white lilies on the mantelpiece, the narrow bed with its bright, luxuriant spread.

Bridgie, folding away her good navy jumper, found a three-inch nail rolled into a corner of a drawer and put it into a cup. Ned always said you never knew when you might want a three-inch nail.

She washed her face and feet and dried them tentatively with pale blue towels embroidered with paler rosebuds and knelt before the Child of Prague to say her rosary. On the far side of the wall her grandsons slept. Edward, tall and blonde, and David, who had Ned's grey eyes, his slow, half-reluctant smile.

Eamonn, just back from a month in Brussels, sat on Bridgie's pretty, flowered settee. His hand-made shoes reflected in the polished floorboards were as soft and supple as gloves. Claudia hadn't waited for his return. She was in town having lunch with friends. A previous engagement, she explained to Bridgie, Eamonn would understand. Bridgie, pouring tea, thought of Ned going into the town for the messages, she waiting for his return with the floor swept, a good fire, the kettle boiled. For weeks after his death she'd been afraid to leave the house, terrified against all reason that he might somehow return and find the fire dead, the door shut against him.

She asked Eamonn to find out the time of daily Mass. She wanted him to put a few nails in the walls and hang up her pictures that she brought from home. Later, he gave her a leaflet showing the times of church services. Four Masses every morning, six on Sundays. She put the leaflet in the back of her prayer book, faintly scandalised by this proliferation of Masses.

She saw her grandchildren rarely. They drifted in and out of the house - long legged teenagers who spoke with the strange patois of youth - the last words of sentences inflected upwards, like a perennial question.

In a hardware store she asked a pimpled, cox-combed youth for a holy water font. He shrugged helplessly, offered her birdbaths, plastic ponds, gravel –filled dishes with pulsing water bubbles flung up by a small electric pump. He sounded foreign. English, she thought. He might even be a German.

At the Senior Citizens club Bridgie sat beside Miss Daly while a woman with a thin, unyielding body lectured them about the benefits of essential oils.

'*Essential Oils my arse,*' said Miss Daly. '*I'm gasping for a fag.*' She laughed hoarsely, offering sweets from a brown paper bag.

'*Lizzie*', she said. '*Never mind the "Miss". I didn't miss as much as people thought.*'

Lizzie had a room in her niece's house. '*Up under the slates,*' she said cheerfully. '*When there's nothing on the telly I can lie on my backside and admire the stars.*'

The Sheriff Street tenements where she was born were levelled to the ground now, old neighbours scattered to the four winds.

'*Neilstown,*' said Lizzie bitterly, '*Jobstown, Killinarden. The back of Godspeed. I moved out to Clontarf to be with the niece. I give a hand minding the children. We'll get the bus into O'Connell Street in the morning.*'

Claudia, watching them heading for the bus with Bridgie, even in sweltering June, wearing her coat, stockings, heavy laced–up shoes - nicknamed them The Two Musketeers.

Foraging among Camden Street stalls, Lizzie bought Toblerones and satin hair bands -presents for her niece's children.

'*A child's a child,*' she said indulgently. '*They always expect me to bring them back something.*'

They ate a bag of oranges in Stephens Green, Lizzie greedily, wiping the juice from her chin with the corner of her cardigan, Bridgie surreptitiously, behind her cupped hand, and lit candles in Whitefriar Street church and prayed with sibilant fervour, stained glass windows dripping coloured shadows on Lizzie's grey, corrugated curls, Bridgie's gloved and folded hands.

'*At home,*' Bridgie said, '*you wouldn't see a sinner's soul from one day to the next only the postman. The curlew and the blackbird. That's all you'd ever hear in Kiltrasna. The curlew and the blackbird.*'

'*My granny was in O'Connell Street the morning the Rising started,*' said Lizzie, '*you could hear the guns out as far as Swords. Her hearing was never right after, she had only one good ear 'til the day she died.*'

Overnight, it seemed, winter came. Snow fell in a hurried, genteel flurry; footpaths glistened under a treacherous veneer of ice. In Bridgie's flat, hot water gushed enthusiastically from taps; radiators murmured consolingly, the pale walls shuddered delicately against the onslaught of thin, December light.

'*Next Spring,*' Bridgie promised Lizzie, '*we'll go down to Kiltrasna. There's only a bus once a week. If we don't go of a Tuesday we'll have to get McGuire's hackney from the town.*'

'Mrs Denagher? This is Maggie, Lizzie's niece. I'm afraid poor Auntie passed away last night. A heart attack. The funeral is on Friday at ten, burial in Glasnevin. She talked about you a lot - we thought we should let you know.'

The Sacred Heart, The Kennedy's, The Little Flower, De Valera, slumped patiently against the bedroom walls, watched her with luminous, sympathetic eyes.

In the supermarket she bought a pound of ham and a cake with lemon icing.

'You have to bring something,' she told the young Latvian at the checkout, counting coins carefully into the girl's palm. 'You can't go into a wake house with one hand as long as the other.'

A plump woman in jeans opened the front door that was painted a dark, elegant blue.

'Hi, I'm Maggie,' she said,' you must be Mrs Denagher. How very kind of you to call.'

Bridgie sat in the untidy kitchen, the ham, the lemon cake, in a shopping bag on her lap. A cat with neatly coiled tail sat in a pool of sunlight, watching her with green, perceptive eyes.

She wondered which room they had laid Lizzie's body out in, the good front room maybe, or up under the skylight, her sightless eyes searching a sky without stars.

She put her gifts awkwardly on the table beside her and then stood and hovered grimly until the woman, with sudden understanding, ushered her briskly into the hall.

'Door on the left,' she said, 'I'll just switch on the light for you first.'

Bridgie stood, bewildered, in a cloakroom painted the luscious purple of a ripe plum. A picture of a naked woman hung over the door, her curves a mere suggestion of broad brushstrokes in magenta and old rose, her nipples, small splashes of a paler pink, matched exactly the colour of the towel cupped on a porcelain hook that was shaped like a servile, supplicating hand.

'*It says 'house private.'* Claudia's voice was shrill with embarrassed outrage. '*The body is in a funeral home - didn't you see it on the paper?'*

At the funeral Mass the church was almost empty, the congregation scattered through the high, echoing building like a handful of flung stones. People wandered around the side altars, lighting candles, kneeling in private prayer. A young woman with a flat, oriental face photographed a stained–glass window. The priest droned on, mesmerised by the sound of his own sonorous voice. In a discreet corner of the graveyard a JCB grumbled to itself, impatient at the enforced wait.

Lizzie's niece stood decorously, with bowed head, a brash puddle of lilies and carnations in her outstretched arms. When the coffin was lowered she sighed and placed her wreath into the undertaker's waiting hands as her children raised denim-clad arms and flung a scarlet shower of single, plastic-wrapped roses into the open grave.

Bridgie swathed The Sacred Heart, John and Jacqueline Kennedy, De Valera, the Little Flower, in the folds of her crossover apron and wedged them securely in the bottom of her suitcase.

'*Not even a decade of the Rosary,'* she confided bitterly to the Child of Prague as she swaddled him in her good, interlock vest.

'*Funeral parlours. Family flowers. She was entitled to a wake. She was good to them children. We're going straight home to Kiltrasna in the morning. House private, my arse.*'

CINNAMON TOAST

'Anybody home?'

My heart sinks at the sound of Eve's voice but before I can even begin to tidy the worst of the debris from the breakfast table she appears in the kitchen doorway. The place looks a mess. Breakfast dishes are piled in the sink. There are crumbs on the draining board and every flaw in my old-fashioned, cluttered kitchen is cruelly floodlit by the low winter sun.

Eve looks wonderful, as usual. Her makeup and hair are flawless. Her pure white sweater is probably cashmere, her leather boots shine like newly fallen conkers, her trousers fit like a second skin. I fill the kettle, wishing I'd found time to put on lipstick, wishing I was wearing something more flattering than my oldest jeans and an oversized jumper with the elbows worn through.

Our tiny Jack Russell, Tyson, who has been snoring gently on the rocking chair which he considers to be his own exclusive property, opens one eye and growls softly as he rearranges himself with his head buried pointedly in his paws. Eve ignores him - ever since she inherited Bird Cottage from her grandmother, Molly, and became our nearest neighbour - Eve and Tyson have treated each other with mutual contempt.

'Clever old me,' Eve says as she sits down and flips open the glossy magazine she is carrying. *'You can stop worrying, Jenny - look at what I've just discovered.'*

She points with a perfectly manicured fingernail to a caption that reads *'PENELOPE ALBRIGHT DESIGNS YOUR PERFECT CHRISTMAS.'*

I stare at the image of a Christmas tree which stands in a wood-panelled, firelit hall. The tree is decorated entirely in maroon and gold and the gracefully curving staircase behind it is swagged with branches of greenery tied with matching maroon ribbon. A golden retriever lies underneath, his coat gleaming in the reflected firelight.

'Doesn't it look wonderful?' Eve asks. *'Can't you just imagine this in your hallway on Christmas Eve with snow falling outside? Bruce will never have seen anything like it.'*

My stomach does a familiar back flip. Ever since our youngest, Shauna, announced that she would be coming home from New Zealand for Christmas, bringing Bruce with her, I've been feeling slightly sick at the mention of his name. Bruce is our future son-in-law whom we have never met. According to Shauna he is the most handsome, caring, loving man in the universe and we will adore him on sight. We have so much in common. His family are farmers, just like us. The only difference is that Bruce's family farms over three thousand acres – and their house, if the photographs are anything to go by, is slightly larger and a great deal more luxurious than Alderton Park, our local stately home.

'He'll have to take us as he finds us,' said my husband, Phil. *'No use him expecting swimming pools and peacocks on the lawn.'* He reached for another slice of my special lemon cake and winked at me.

'After a few days of your home cooking he won't even notice the wallpaper.'

I glared at him and pushed the cake tin out of reach. Not even a five-starred Michelin chef couldn't blind anyone to the fact that we haven't been able to afford to redecorate in years.

I'd begun to notice the house's shortcomings long before Shauna dropped her bombshell – ever since last Spring, to be precise, when Eve, newly divorced and obviously wealthy, decided to downsize her life and completely revamp the cottage and live there herself. Suddenly there were builders and landscape gardeners and interior decorators crawling all over the place. And then, just as suddenly, about six months ago they all disappeared, leaving a miniature Ideal Home behind them.

At Eve's housewarming I stood in a corner, trying my best to look inconspicuous and feeling frumpish and ill-at ease in my best linen shift, gaping like an idiot at what had once been the bottom half of Molly's tiny, two up, two down cottage. The poky downstairs had miraculously become a stylish, light filled space with silvery grey walls and delicate wrought iron steps that spiralled up from a pale polished floor. The untidy cottage garden was gone and now double doors led onto a gravelled terrace where a stone cherub balanced on one chubby leg in the middle of a white marble fountain. The whole place looked like something out of the Sunday supplements and I mentally compared it with our own shabby farmhouse - the mismatched furniture, the washing machine that groaned like a sulky teenager every time it was asked to wash a shirt, the kitchen range that behaved beautifully for months and then-just for the hell of it- decided to cremate an entire Christmas dinner for ten.

'Landscape gardening, my eye,' Phil said as we walked up the lane together afterwards. *'It's nothing but a few shrubs and a bit of gravel. And as for that cherub thingy with the water dribbling downs its chin-reminds me more of a teething baby than an angel.'*

So I should have known what to expect when I began to drop hints about our big old-fashioned kitchen with its cracked tiles and amateurish looking cupboards. Phil, who belongs to the 'if it ain't broke don't fix it' school of thought, acted as if I'd gone mad.

'*My father built those cupboards,*' he said, '*none of your chipboard there. Solid oak, they are - every inch.*'

I tried to explain all this to Eve but she's just as bad as Phil. My future son-in-law, who has grown up in the New Zealand's answer to Southfork, is coming for Christmas, the place is a mess and neither of them can see that we have a problem-which is mostly money, or lack of it.

'*This is such a lovely old house,*' Eve says airily, '*all it needs is a bit of TLC and imagination and a lick of paint - it's got oodles of character.*'

I look at her smugly smiling face and want to shout that I hate character. I'm sick and tired of character. I want a cooker with a thermostat that works. I want matching dining room chairs. I want a sofa that doesn't threaten to swallow me whole, like Jonah's whale, every time I sit down to put my feet up.

But Eve has no intention of giving up – by afternoon she's back, armed with a sheaf of paint charts. '*I picked these up in town,*' she says as she fans them briskly in front of me. '*If you're going to redecorate we haven't much time-it's almost the middle of November already.*'

I am beginning to suspect that life in a country village isn't all that my new neighbour imagined – she's forever popping in on some pretext or other. Only yesterday she confessed that although she loves her little cottage she still misses her beautiful house and the antique furniture she and her ex-husband collected together and which was sold when they divorced. '*It's not the money,*' she said bitterly, '*it's the memories. How could he? We bought some of those things on our honeymoon. Men just don't understand that some things are priceless.'*

As I rinse her coffee mug and dry it on a decidedly threadbare tea towel and mentally add a dozen replacements to an already overstretched shopping list, I think resentfully that some people are never happy. Still- I know she means well so I sigh and pick up a chart of varying shades of beige and pretend to study it.

'Cinnamon Toast looks nice.'

Eve dismisses Cinnamon Toast with barely a glance. *'Much too dull,'* she says briskly.

'How about something really dramatic for a change? This Molten Gold would look wonderful with terracotta tiles and plain linen blinds.'

I stare at the small square of sludgy, mustard yellow as she waves a disdainful hand towards the windows. *'And these curtains will definitely have to go for a start.'*

Phil comes in from milking and Eve stands up and stacks the paint charts tidily together and gives them a brisk little pat and smiles flirtatiously at my husband.

'Hello, Phil-you look worn out, poor man –been up since dawn as usual, I suppose.'

'It's what farmers do.' Phil smiles back at Eve and kisses me absentmindedly on the cheek.

'Any chance of a coffee, love - it's freezing out?'

He sits down in the chair Eve has just vacated and begins to leaf idly through the charts. *'Golden Dawn, Buttercup Kiss, Texas Rose.'* He snorts. *'Who thinks up these ridiculous names? They all look the same anyway. Why not just call them yellow and be done with it?'*

Behind his back Eve raises her eyebrows wryly and smiles.

'Men,' the smile says. *'Aren't they impossible sometimes?'*

It's begun to snow - it's already nearly dark although it's only four o'clock in the afternoon. Phil offers Eve a lift home, he has to go into town for a part for the tractor, which, naturally, is going to cost another small fortune. We could have bought a villa in the sun for the amount of money we've spent on that tractor over the years.

Bang goes my new curtains-not to mention my terracotta tiles.

I pour myself a defiant glass of sherry and settle myself in the rocking chair with Eve's magazine. Tyson, sighing resignedly at this disruption to his routine, falls asleep on my foot. The magazine is not one I have ever bought for myself – it's full of advertisements for clothes by designers whose names I can hardly pronounce and photographs of Charity Balls and Polo Tournaments and Society weddings being attended by Very Important People that I have never even heard of. I've certainly never heard of Penelope Albright. But in the world of Society weddings and Charity Balls what Penelope says obviously goes and when it comes to Christmas decorations she certainly pulls no punches. Be ruthless, she admonishes sternly. Go through your existing decorations and discard anything that looks dated. Choose a colour scheme and **stick to it.** Get rid of multi-coloured tree lights. Don't even think of tinsel.

I look around me at the faded wallpaper, threadbare rugs, and mismatched furniture. I think of peacocks and swimming pools. I think of Eve's pale polished floors and deep couches and pearly grey walls. If Penelope Albright can be ruthless then so can I will be pitiless, a woman without mercy. The way I feel right now I can be the reincarnation of Genghis Khan. Boadicea or Attila the Hun aren't even in my league. Penelope Albright would be proud of me. I'll just go into town tomorrow and order the biggest tree I can find and buy dozens of maroon velvet bows and those pretty, tiny white lights that look like stars and next week, just before Shauna comes home, I'll bake those cute little ginger biscuits (recipe page 253) and tie them to the branches with matching satin ribbon. Then I remember last Christmas when Shauna brought a box of old -fashioned candy canes back from one of her New York trips and hung them on the Christmas tree, and I decide to pass on the ginger biscuits. The candy canes lasted all of ten minutes before Tyson found them. He'd eaten at least a dozen before he was discovered in the garden, being violently sick in a flowerbed.

I've just hauled the last box of decorations down from the attic when Phil phones. The roads are pretty bad but at least the snow has stopped and he's on his way home. The tractor part was a lot cheaper than he thought. He thinks I could do with some cheering up so he's bought a bottle of wine. He sounds tired and I remember with a pang that he's been up since dawn tending a sick animal.

I put the casserole in the oven and set the table and begin to open the boxes. The knitted crib was always the children's favourite Christmas plaything - Joseph and Mary were regularly press-ganged into making guest appearances at teddy bears picnics or Ken and Barbie weddings. And though the sheep bear a striking resemblance to Rothweiller puppies I'm sure that Penelope would agree that the whole thing has a certain folksy charm.

I think I'll keep the crib.

A stuffed felt robin that looks like a misshapen plum pudding on legs once won first prize (two balloons and a colouring book) for its creator in senior infants.

Not the robin then.

The cheap, plastic baubles painted with snow scenes were bought with carefully hoarded pocket money at a mid - summer jumble sale in the village hall and were presented to me, packed in an old egg carton, by two anxious small girls as a special present for my July birthday.

I can't possibly get rid of the baubles.

Nobody has ever admitted responsibility for the fairy's unfortunate punk haircut. And even though it causes her cardboard crown to continuously slip down over one eye, giving her the look of a drunken fishwife, the Christmas tree somehow wouldn't be the same without her.

The ropes of tarnished gold and silver beads were a gift from my mother. A tiny Cinderella once insisted on wearing them in the school concert and managed to trip up half the cast in the grand finale as a result.

And now I'm smiling as I rediscover homemade cards and cotton wool snowmen and the Christmas bells made from milk bottle tops and beads.

I'm keeping them-my tatty snowmen and cherubs with backsides rubbed bare of gold paint from the attentions of little fingers.

Because Eve is absolutely right. And Penelope Albright is an idiot. Some things are so precious that they are absolutely priceless.

THE LISTENERS

Matt sits by the window, absorbed in his evening newspaper. In the rocking chair beside him, Ella cradles a blue and white patchwork cushion in her hands, mindlessly counting the regiments of stitches that march endlessly along blue cotton roads. Water drips from a tap in a sudden, agitated flurry and the clock ticks fretfully and then pings with silvery politeness and the dog stirs and sighs in his sleep. Her mind sifts these details and stows them tidily away as she silently chooses words and rejects them again just as quickly, like a fussy, cost-conscious housewife at her shopping.

The dull ache that she has carried in her guts for weeks stirs warningly, waiting to strike and she shivers and wraps her arms around her body, hugging herself for comfort.

'I've lost nearly a stone in the last month.'

Matt, absorbed in the fate of his favourite football club, glances at her briefly, a small frown on his smooth, handsome face.

'Isn't that what you wanted - you said yourself that you could do with losing a few inches.'

'Not like this. At the rate I'm going I'll have disappeared altogether by Christmas.'

She smiles with determined cheerfulness and he returns the smile and then goes back to the sports page and gives a small grunt of annoyance at what he reads there. Bloody selectors haven't the brains of a rocking horse between them. Never can get a damn thing right-he has a good mind to write to the paper. And the Club chairman.

'You look fine to me.' He glances at her again. *'If you're worried you should get George to have a look at you.'*

She clenches her hands in her lap and watches a spider abseil nonchalantly down the sheer, white face of the refrigerator where it swings to and fro, to and fro until, suddenly, tiring of the limelight, it drops abruptly at her feet and scurries away into the darkness.

'Get George to have a look at you.' As if she was an old washing machine that had outlasted its usefulness.

The round- faced clock smiles luminously at Ella from the table by her bedside as it chips patiently at the hours to be endured before dawn. She lies rigidly beside her sleeping husband, watching the headlights of passing cars play tag across the ceiling before they slither down the walls like living things and disappear under the skirting boards. Sometimes, lying like this, she imagines a vast pool of light underneath the house, an undiscovered ocean that will someday spill over and engulf her. She reaches over and touches her husband's out- flung hand for comfort but Matt grunts in his sleep and turns pettishly away.

She rises noiselessly, solicitous of the sleeping stranger in her bed.

Down the hall, in her pink and white bedroom, Miranda restlessly kicks away the blankets that cover her long, beautiful limbs and sighs deeply, smiling to herself in her dreams.

In their hive, hidden deep in the laurel hedge, the bees drowse and wait patiently for the dawn.

In the kitchen Ella makes tea and takes it into the garden where she sits huddled under the cherry tree in a white, plastic chair, listening to a neighbour's dog howling its defiance to the moon.

George Harwell M.D. leans back in his padded, leather chair and steeples his manicured fingers smugly across his chest. He and Matt have known each other since college. They golf together occasionally. Twice a year they dine in each other's houses. Ella has come to dread these occasions. She has never felt entirely at ease with George or his expensive, beige wife.

'Nothing much wrong as far as I can see. Of course, with women of your age things can begin to act up a bit.'

He presses the intercom on his desk and smiles reassuringly.

'We'll get the Prof to give us a second opinion- just in case. I'll get Jane to fix you up with an appointment.'

When he shakes hands, his gold cuff links wink comfortingly at her as if inviting her to share in some secret joke.

On her way through the outer office, Jane, George's receptionist, hands her a heavy cream envelope.

'Your appointment, Mrs Cantwell, Professor Donaldson can fit you in on the sixth. Twelve noon.'

Jane's cashmere sweater purrs complacently across her perky, perfect breasts.

She smiles at Ella, silently inviting admiration for her delicately enunciated vowels, her consonants that are carefully pruned to an elegant blandness - like a woman displaying an Aubusson rug to a less affluent neighbour.

Miranda, in the throes of first, unrequited teenage love, rushes off in the usual flurry of mislaid homework and slammed doors.

'Bye, Mum, hope it's not twins.'

And down the path with her long hair flying and careless kisses tossed behind her on the busy air.

Matt straightens his tie and smiles at himself in the mirror behind Ella's shoulder.

'Might be a bit late this evening, I'm having lunch with old Randell.'

'Will you be in home in time for dinner?'

One corner of his mouth lifts as if preparing to smile at some secret joke and then changes its mind again and settles back into an expression of proper, husbandly concern.

'Probably. Your appointment is for twelve, you said? '

'Yes.'

'Oh, it'll be nothing. Old George says it's really just a formality. Just to be on the safe side. You know what a fusspot he can be sometimes.'

Let's hear it for good old George.

The garden waits in respectful silence, holding its breath as Ella, feeling slightly foolish, hunkers down in the lavender and confides her secret terror to her friends, the bees.

The bees are silent, listening with rapt attention, seesawing on the rims of summer roses.

Ella dresses carefully, applies lipstick and eye shadow and then opens the bathroom cabinet, and gathers the little bottles of pills that march along the shelf in gleaming, self-important rows. Tonight, she promises herself silently, when the Professor has laughed her out of her foolishness, they will build a bonfire, Ella and Matt and Miranda, and consign her redundant voodoo charms to the flames.

Miranda sits at her desk and absently runs her fingers along edge of her ruler as she watches Ben from under lowered lashes. The history teacher drones on about the Napoleonic Wars. When she catches Ben's eye she turns away and tosses her head disdainfully, like an impatient pony but when she turns around again he is leaning towards blonde, curvy, giggly Samantha, his body shielding Samantha from the sudden, sweet malevolence of Miranda's smile.

A fly sits on the edge of the desk, flexing its thread – like legs one by one, like a can-can dancer warming up for the grand finale of the show.

Miranda brings the ruler down.

Splat!

Ella rides up to the Professor's consulting rooms in a glass lift with a heavily made-up woman who, despite the heat, is swathed in furs. She returns the woman's genteel, social smile and wishes she could bury her face in the glossy, dead skin and burrow for comfort in the musky animal scent of the woman's coat.

Matt smiles at his secretary as he gathers documents into his briefcase with a practiced flick.

'Care for a bit of lunch?'

The girl nods, her pretty pink mouth curving with pleasure.

The lift purrs softly and she leans against the protection of his shoulder, admiring her myriad reflections in its mirrored walls. Tomorrow, aiming for a more sophisticated image, she plans to have her hair restyled.

In this town image is everything.

The Professor taps Ella's X-rays with his gold- plated pen and purses his lips.

'I can't really tell conclusively from these. It may be nothing.'

He slides the file into a drawer but not before she sees the legend that is printed on the cover under her name. **Not to be seen by the patient.**

He leans towards her confidingly, like a small boy sharing a grubby secret.

'I'm sending you to see Mr Briody. Absolutely top man. No harm in letting him have a look at you.'

Hysteria threatens and she chokes down sudden laughter as she imagines herself drawn up in the forecourt of some greasy garage while The Professor and George and the Top Man crowd around her craning their necks as she lies with the flap of her stomach neatly folded back like the bonnet of a second-hand car.

The Professor looks up sharply at the sound, watchful for any signs of any unseemly emotion.

'I'll let your own doctor have a full report in due course.'

He dismisses her, shaking her hand with cold, oddly calloused fingers.

In the flowerbeds that edge the car park the shrubs wear their names inscribed in Latin on tags around their necks, like delegates at some obscure convention.

The opulent cars wait patiently, row upon row, bright as serried tin soldiers. Butterflies hover disdainfully over well-bred perennials and then just for the hell of it, decide to slum it on a clump of nettles in a forgotten corner. A cigarette packet lurks under a zinnia bush, poking its tongue out with disrespectful glee at the carefully tended lawns.

Ella reverses her car carefully and drives home, rigid with terror.

In the classroom, a stray sunbeam makes a dusty highway between the window and the smug, self-satisfied face of the clock that hangs above the door. Amanda feels she will die of sheer happiness as she returns Ben's smile.

The Professor takes Ella's file from a drawer, sighs and considers phoning Mr.Briody. Then the pretty carriage clock on his desk chimes the hour and he replaces the file and phones his secretary instead.

'Marion dear? I'm leaving now. Look after things for me like a good girl.'

As his car bullies its way through early evening traffic he selects a tape and listens to a famous actor reading an impassioned extract from Ulysses. It's been a tough day - he's glad it's over.

He relaxes as the actor's voice pours over him like melted chocolate.

The Professor is very fond of James Joyce.

The bee is dying, trapped in the saucer full of treacle that Ella had left near the picnic table to snare the wasps. With the hollow of a spoon she scrapes the little creature up and lays it gently in the lavender-scented dimness of the flowerbed. Its iridescent wings are dull and ragged, like shreds of torn tissue.

'Don't die,' she prays with silent desperation, *'I'm so sorry-please don't die.'*

The bee hums wearily as it crawls with infinite patience towards the shelter of the lilac bushes, trailing its ruined wings behind it in the dust.

Matt stares out the window and watches a jet plane arrowing towards the South. He pictures Ella's tired face. Still, old George had been right. He feels a sudden spurt of gratitude for George. He'd have gone with Ella today - if she'd asked him. Too damn stubborn by half - that was always Ella's trouble.

The jet becomes a speck and vanishes, leaving only an undecipherable scribble of vapour against the blue to mark its passing.

The sound of the phone ringing shatters the garden's honey coloured silence.

'*Hello?*'

'*Hi, it's Matt. How did it go with the Professor?*'

He's not sure,' she says,' *but he seems to thinks it nothing very serious.*'

'*I knew you were worrying about nothing*'.

His voice is suddenly buttery with indulgent love.

'*It seems this Ben has finally noticed our daughter's existence. She's watching him play football after school. I said you wouldn't mind.*'

'*No, I don't mind.*'

His voice changes again.

'*I'll be late this evening love. Things are hectic here. See you about nine.*'

'Love.' He hasn't called her love in years.

Ella lies in scented bath water and watches sun-dappled shadows dancing across her belly and thighs. When the water is almost cold she rises and dresses with care in a blue silk dress that she has hardly ever worn. She pours wine into a delicate glass and carefully she carries it and her little bottles out into the sunshine.

The bee lies where she left it, unmoving, like a scrap of dusty velvet.

Love. Matt called her 'love'. Suddenly she brings her heel down with savage strength, weeping as she grinds the small brown body into the dust.

She sinks to her knees as a robin quicksteps up the path and stops a few feet away, watching her with bright, knowing eyes. A pair of ants track towards her and consult together briefly before scurrying away again into the darkness.

The bees hum softly to each other, ignoring her existence.

She begins to open the little bottles, one by one.

WATCHMAN, WHAT OF THE NIGHT?

Three weeks ago the paper shop, the last occupied building in an almost derelict street, was sold to the developers. For over two years the owner held out for his price - now he is moving to Dubrovnik. Yesterday he watched impassively as the bulldozers moved in. By the summer he will be gone and teams of young men with strange accents and tired faces will have transformed the shabby old building into the newest link in a chain of hotels that stretch into Europe and beyond.

Nora, who for thirty-six years stood behind the counter - tutting impatiently over schoolchildren's painstakingly counted pennies or nodding respectfully to a succession of Parish Priests collecting their morning newspapers, watched without regret as the shop and the cheerless bed-sit above it where she has spent all her working life collapsed in on itself with a dusty, muffled sigh.

Nora has earned the right to a new beginning, to the comfort of unshadowed corners and warm, sunlit rooms. She has already paid a deposit on an apartment in one of the newly converted warehouses down by the river.

She sits by the window in a café and smiles with practised flirtatiousness at a commercial traveller at the next table. But she is only half-aware of the stranger, she is thinking of other things. Her new home will have a fitted kitchen in pale oak, a balcony wide enough to hold a sunshade and two plastic chairs. She is leaving her quiet backstreet of boarded up houses and vagrant shadows for a place where the loneliness of night will be banished by streetlights, neon signs, the reassuring searchlights of passing cars. She will be surrounded by sunlight glinting seductively on water, the sounds of footsteps, music, and laughter. She, too, will become a part of the muted gaiety of the world just outside her door.

Kate, her mother, died young. Her father lingered on for thirty years, sharing the small isolated farmhouse with taciturn, shy, hardworking Uncle Con, his only brother.

Before he died, Grandfather, that dour Puritan, disinherited Con, the poet-singer, in favour of Joshua, her diligent, joyless father. Con never married. He stayed and worked the land alongside his brother. He treated Kate with quiet, almost servile, courtesy. He addressed her as 'Ma'am,' as if she were the lady of some fine house, his master's wife.

Now Nora is selling the farmhouse and farm. She has already found a new home for Con in Mountain View Crescent. The Crescent's residents, Senior Citizens of a world that has somehow moved on without them, have each been culled from their separate solitudes by Social Services, Health Boards, concerned relatives-good people who are anxious to build a caring, inclusive society under the Celtic Tiger's benevolent, indulgent gaze.

The Crescent is a box-like enclosure of small, identical pebble-dashed houses that have sprung up two miles outside the town on a sour, scrubby field that, until tax incentives made it too good an opportunity to miss, had been neglected and uncultivated for years.

The little houses of Mountain View have been very carefully planned. But the name is misleading - for the mountain is miles away, a thumb smudge that is barely visible against the horizon. Still, each of the twenty four kitchens, painted in sunshine yellow, is angled to catch the sun. They each have low cupboards, wipe clean surfaces, a rocking chair drawn up to the fake flames of the small electric fire. There are security cameras and a resident warden. The communal gardens have pale gravelled paths and plastic birdbaths cleverly painted and moulded to look like weathered stone.

Twenty-four red geraniums in white, plastic pots made a defiant slash of gaiety against white, plastic front doors, like too-bright lipstick on an ageing spinster's face.

Con will have plenty of company. There is Miss Aggie Smyth, a retired priest's housekeeper who lives in number 24. Aggie, giddy with the freedom of being released at last from the dull decorum of her past, wears gaily-coloured cotton dresses, cardigans with pearl buttons, silky stockings that give her legs an oily, reflective sheen. She spends her days baking porter cakes and gingerbread and apple tarts for the priests who - despite their many promises - are far too busy to call.

At number 26, Mrs Brennan, the reclusive widow of a schoolmaster, bitter at her loss of social standing, spurns Miss Smyth's unwanted cakes. She is diabetic, she never eats sweet things, the sugar would kill her. She closes her door resolutely, shutting out Miss Smyth's gingerbread and apple pies, her foolish, bewildered smiles.

'*I don't want to go into that place Nora.*' said Con.

She ignores him, guiltily producing small gifts and laying them on the kitchen table - forty cigarettes, chocolate, *Ireland's Own*, an apple cake.

'The Crescent is lovely, Uncle Con. Central heating and neighbours beside you and an alarm button in every room in case you get sick in the night. You won't know yourself.'

When she leaves, he walks down with her down the laneway that is hardly more than a cart track - a ribbon of stunted grass between twin lines of rutted stones.

'We always reared great hay in these fields,' Con says. Nora smiles at the memory of her father leading the horses, the swathes of fresh grass falling behind the mowing machine, herself tagging behind Con like a tenacious shadow as he turned the green swathes face upwards to the sun. She remembers her mother, Kate, coming down the lane carrying their dinner in a basket, wearing a dress that was patterned with faded washed out roses. They ate under the shadow of the sally bushes that lined the riverbanks. Her father waded into the shallows and washed the sweat from his face and arms and Con struck a match and lit her mother's cigarette and then his own, his cupped hands cradling the guttering flame.

'Go on, Con, sing a song for us.'
'Sing Mammy's song, Uncle Con.'

'I'll take you home again Kathleen
Across the ocean wild and wide.'

The child, Nora, entranced by his deep, beautiful voice, pressing herself against his arm, watching her mother's smiling face and the changing lights in her quiet eyes.

The young man driving the taxi that took Con away was tall and blonde with pale blue eyes and high, Slavic cheekbones. The cobbles outside the kitchen door were already sprouting weeds -dandelion and dock and daisies with bright, innocent hearts. Con stood by the open barn door and stared into its motionless, shadowy depths.

'*Seventy six years,*' he said, '*seventy six years, man and boy.*'

The young man didn't answer. He has very little English. Unless people speak slowly and clearly, he seldom understands.

The car passed along a once-familiar landscape where rows and rows of identical houses spilled and overflowed along once - quiet country lanes. The old school was gone, and the dancehall with its galvanised roof.

'*I wouldn't know the place,*' said Con.' *I might as well be a stranger.*'

He stared out the car window at apartment blocks, restaurants - Italian,Thai,Chinese-boutiques,banks, book shops, shopping centres - all swaggering along arm-in-arm on either side of the elegant, cobble-locked promenades and newly widened roads. Even the derelict warehouses down by the riverbank which lay empty and neglected since he was a boy had been reclaimed, the walls mercilessly chiselled and sandblasted down to their bare, granite bones.

The auctioneer, face beaming and hand outstretched, crossed the farmyard with quick, business-like strides. He carried a clipboard and a tape measure in a round, metal casing.

'*Nora.*' He greeted her like a long-lost friend. '*God, it's quiet up here.*' he said, '*but it seems to be what they all want nowadays -to get away from it all.*'

He glanced around approvingly at well-clipped hedges, barn doors freshly painted. He liked a place that was well looked after. It made it easier to shift.

He stuck his head into the barn and squinted at the rafters, ran his hands over the pure craftsmanship of the cut stone whitewashed walls and followed Nora into the house, scribbling busily as he went. Many original features intact, he noted, and listed them in a quick almost illegible scrawl; the kitchen hearth with its soot-stained chimneybreast, the black, fat-bellied iron kettle that hung above it, the small, uncurtained deep-set windows, the uneven stone-flagged floor. Peace, he wrote, tranquillity, panoramic views of the surrounding countryside, scribble, scribble, scribble. The clichés tumbled eagerly from the tip of his silver -plated pen.

He raised his eyes at the smallness of the rooms as he unwound the tape measure and gave one end to Nora to hold. He measured, knocked knowledgeably on walls, and admired the fireplace in the shadowed front parlour, the heavy table balancing sturdily on a barley sugar leg, the oil lamp with a painted, glass shade.

'*We could do with a bit of light in here,*' and he pulled back the yellowed lace curtains. Light puddled on the lino-covered floor.

Outside again, he made mundane enquires about acreage and boundaries.

'*You'll make a right packet on this Nora- they'll be queuing up for it. You should hold on to the few acres. They'll be worth twice as much again in a few years' time - aren't they re-zoning this whole side of the town, out as far as the flax mill?*'

By six o'clock Con Leahy, surrounded by his belongings, sits motionless in the kitchen of 23

Mountain View Crescent, his hands folded in his lap as he stares at the buttery, yellow walls that glow in the pale, vindictive radiance of a low winter sun.

Captain Mahon in Number 22 has already called to welcome Con. He brings leaflets and informs Con briskly of the fire drills, whist nights, outings to places of scenic beauty and historical interest, which he organises and oversees on behalf of the other residents. Captain Mahon is used to being in command. He has seen service in the Congo. He once stood in guards-of-honour for presidents and Popes. He has marched behind the coffins of statesmen and shouted terse, instantly -obeyed commands to platoons of white-gloved soldiers.

A man with a badge pinned firmly to the left breast of his uniform jacket which says. **WALTER CALDER - WARDEN** in black, no-nonsense script, knocks on Con's door and, using his own key, enters.

'Have you met the neighbours yet?' he asks as he draws the curtains closed against the night.

'Lovely people. You won't know yourself with the company. Everyone is friends here. We all look out for each other. But keep the curtains closed as soon as it gets dark, the world isn't what it was. You never know who might be watching.'

Walter's handshake is reassuring. His eyes, beaming kindly through thick, round rimmed glasses give him the appearance of a freshly–landed trout.

The auctioneer sits in the hotel bar which his wife often jokingly refers to as his second home. He hasn't a minute to call his own. Business is good; the whole town is expanding – bursting apart at the seams, like a snake shedding a too- tight skin. That wee house and bit of land he saw today – he has a client in mind for it already, a man like himself who can see the possibilities of putting a few bob into it before selling it on again. In his mind, he calculates the cost. Power hose the cobbles, put out a table and a few chairs and there's your patio. A bit of timber decking to give a view of the river-even if it's only a glimmer in the distance. A water view is a water view. It'll add thousands to the price.

The auctioneer orders another drink and settles down for the evening in the comfortable familiarity of wood-panelled walls, frosted windows, the bawdy wink of brandy, gin, ruby port, lined up on narrow, polished shelves.

Street lamps beam benignly down on Mountain View Crescent where Warden Calder patrols round the concrete paths that are bathed in sickly, yellow light.

Miss Aggie Smyth in Number 24 lies sleepless, remembering the dim graciousness of high, shadowed rooms, starched linen, fine crystal, the priests and prelates whose wellbeing was once entrusted to her care.

Captain Mahon irons his shirt and polishes his boots, brushes his jacket free of lint. He folds newspapers and re-arranges the books on his bedside shelf in neat, serried rows.

Once a soldier, always a soldier.

In Number 23, Con sits in his rocking chair. His features, slack with sleep, slide into each other like melting snow. He dreams of a woman in a flower-patterned dress. She is standing in a shadowed room, leaning against a door that is latched securely against the night. Her lips move silently as she sings to herself the words of a familiar, well-loved song.

The curtains are undrawn.

The little windows are full of sky.

41

I BELIEVE IN ANGELS

'What's that bloody smell?'

'It's a scented candle that Maggie gave me- she thought it might relax me.'

'Scented candle, my arse - you'll burn the house down between the pair of you before you're finished.'

He's a good man, my Christy. Works every hour God sends. Gone from early morning, winter or summer. Sometimes I don't see him 'til after dark. It could be lonesome enough at times. Never bothered to mix much with the neighbours before Maggie came. Not my sort. Breeding like rabbits the lot of them. Scatters of snot-nosed kids and lines of grey washing in every back garden with the track of a child's arse still on the sheets.

We have none of our own. Twenty years married and not a sign. My fault, his fault, God's fault-what difference does it make? Round and round the finger goes and where it's pointing no one knows. Christy won't go near a doctor.

'None of their bloody business,' he says, *'aren't we all right as we are? You have to play the hand you're dealt.'*

Christy can't stand Maggie with her red lipstick and her tight skirts and her bad language.

Rich-coming from Christy that could light wet turf with his swearing.

'It doesn't sound right,' he says. *'No man likes to hear that sort of language coming from a woman.'*

There's no man cluttering up Maggie's life, that's for sure.

'*Once is enough to be caught,*' she tells me. '*I got shut of one no-good bastard year ago. Why would I want to be going back to all that hardship? No woman in her right mind wants to be bothered wasting the best years of her life being a bloody servant for a waster. Worn out before her time washing and cleaning and scrimping and saving the few bob he brings home after he's finished with the pub and the bookie. A kid every twelve months. What does she get out of it? Varicose veins. Stretch marks. Tits like tired balloons when the party's over.*'

Easy for Maggie to talk. An independent woman with her own house. A car. Plenty of money. New clothes any time she wants them. A bit of a puzzle all the same. Talking like she hates men, dresses like she can't do without them. Tight skirts, tight jumpers. Tight little arse.

'*Great arse,*' says Christy, '*pity about the rest of her. The woman's astray in the head. All that New Age bullshit. Feng shui, essential oils, angels. God give me patience.*'

'*You're as mad as a March hare,*' Christy says. '*you and your feckin' angels. The next thing you'll be telling me is you believe in Santy Claus.*'

Laughing down into her face. His eyes dancing. Lovely brown eyes my Christy has, like bog water in the sun.

Maggie only laughs back up at him, her empty wine glass cupped in her two hands.

'*You're a stubborn blind bastard, Christy Moran. You wouldn't notice Satan himself if he landed in your lap.*'

Christy filling up her glass again, wine scribbling a red stain on my good tablecloth.

'*If he landed in your lap girl, you'd know fine well how to welcome him. He wouldn't go back to hell for a month.*'

I don't know what I did with all the hours in the days before Maggie came. Kept the house clean, did the bit of shopping, looked after the garden. Christy likes a tidy house.

She moved in of a Monday morning. When I went out to peg out the washing she was sitting on the front wall in her high heels and tight jeans and red painted toenails, drinking beer from a can and chatting up the removal men.

The next morning she hopped over the back wall and rapped on the kitchen window with her arms full of flowers.

'I'm your new neighbour,' she said. *'Have you the kettle on? I'm only dying for a cigarette and a good chat.'*

Made me laugh, Maggie did. Always something new. Silver nail polish, fake tan, chains around her ankle. The coal man fancies her. Nice chap. Obliging. Been calling round here for years. Always comes in for a drink at Christmastime. Good-looking man, too. Tall, nice eyes. A woman could do a lot worse.

Sometime she asks him in but mostly she just peeps through the lace curtain in my front room and laughs at the sight of him rapping on her front door with a handkerchief round his knuckles for fear he'd smudge the knocker.

'Give him a go, Maggie,' says Christy, *'you'd never know what you'd find under the soot.'*

'I had enough of men to last me a lifetime,' she spits back at him. *'There's more to life than being a stripe on some bastard's mattress. Sex. Romance. Moonlight and roses - bullshit the lot of it. Not worth the trouble.'*

Her voice glittery with spite.

'*It's different for you,*' she tells me. '*There's not many as lucky as you and your Christy.*'

Me and my Christy. That's how it used to be. Only now there's another woman in my man's life. Not a screed of proof. No funny phone calls or bills for flowers in his breast pocket. Christy wouldn't buy a woman flowers until she was in her coffin. Maggie thinks I'm mad.

'*Are you out of your head?*' she says, '*doesn't the whole road know that you're like Darby and Joan, yourself and Christy.*'

Maggie's right. It's all nonsense. Christy with another woman. Don't make me laugh. But you still know - after twenty years you just bloody know. Little things.

'*You go on up to bed, I'll just watch the rest of the news.*' The way he smiles into his own eyes in the bathroom mirror. New shirts with buttoned down collars. Aftershave lotion. Before, it'd be, '*what do I want with that piss?*'

But you have to talk to somebody, else you'd crack up altogether. There's only Maggie to listen to me now. His mother would choke me. Her darling boy? '*God forgive your lying tongue. You should be down on your knees thanking God my Christy ever even looked at you.*'

My own wouldn't be much better. '*You got a good man, isn't he working day and night to keep you in the lap of luxury?*'

Maggie drags me out of the house most days, she says it's to keep me from going off my head. She never gives up, I'll say that for her. Bringing me a new lipstick, a cardigan she doesn't wear, bits of poetry she writes in a child's copybook. I can't understand a word of the poetry. Christy doesn't like the red lipstick.

'*Common looking,*' he says, '*it doesn't look right on a married woman. You're better off with a nice pink.*'

Yesterday it was something else - an ornament to hang on the wall over the bed. Strange looking thing, like a bicycle wheel with feathers. A dream catcher, she called it, invented by the American Indians - it's supposed to catch the bad dreams, the nightmares.

'You're as mad as Maggie,' says Christy. *'You'd believe in anything. An Indian dream-catcher? Try telling that to the Apaches.'*

It didn't me much good anyway. I'm awake since before daylight, heart - scalded with the worry.

'What have you to be worrying about?' Maggie asks. *'You're making yourself sick about nothing. It's all in your mind. Solid as a rock - your Christy.'*

Now she's hanging crystals in the kitchen window to catch the sun. Last week it was wind chimes to channel positive Chi down on his thick head. Makes a joke of it, trying to laugh me out of the terror.

'Ould stick-in-the-mud Christy? The sex symbol of the parish? Christ, Kathleen, would you ever catch yourself on - who'd be bothered?'

A fine looking man like my Christy

Plenty.

He was working late last month - again. It's a long night from ten o'clock. Nothing on telly. Can't sleep. Can't read. Lying there watching the car lights playing cat and mouse across the ceiling. Listening to a dog barking somewhere. The lonesomest sound in the world.

I got up and went downstairs and rang the factory.

'He's not available right now love, he's down on the shop floor.'

The watchman's voice deckled with laughter.

Bastard. Down on the shop floor all right. But with who, with who?

I rang Maggie. Four o'clock in the morning - her voice cobwebby from sleep. The sound of a man's smothered curse when she lifted the receiver. I put down the phone.

Click.

I sat in the front room in the dark, counting the cars going past the gate. The next will be his. The one after. Fifteen, sixteen, seventeen.... thirty......forty.... No Christy.

I never was much of a one for prayer. At the beginning maybe-when I wanted the babies so bad. But when that never happened I just gave up. Never though anyone was listening anyway. Maggie and her bloody angels.

And here I was now, huddled up on the couch frozen to the bone and praying out loud, for God's sake, mumbling the words over and over again like they were the ten times tables.

I must have dropped off. Woke to the sound of something – a rustle like a breeze or a whisper in the dark. I got up and put on the light and opened the curtains and looked out the window. No Christy, no car. Nothing. When I turned my head again that angel was sitting there in the corner of the good couch, wearing some sort of white shimmery stuff, the gold curls tumbling on his shoulders. Wings like snowdrifts. Bare feet with big yellow toenails. I turned out the light and sat down beside him. He never moved, never even turned to look at me. Just sat with his eyes half shut and his head on one side like a blackbird, with the light from the street lamps bouncing off his feathers. Christy and me were grand, I said. No kids, just the two of us. Happy as pigs in shit. Now this woman coming along and destroying everything. Don't know what I'd do without Maggie. Drying my face with the sleeve of my nightdress that was papery with snot. Eyes burned out of me with the crying.

After a while I got up and went up to bed and slept like a child.

When morning came and Christy was home the angel was gone.

He could turn up anywhere - that angel. The coal shed, the kitchen, the car. Never said anything, just listened. He was a great man for listening.

Maggie thought I was cracked. Not much of her fancy talk now.

'Mother of the Divine, Kathleen,' she said, *'you're losing it. Are you still going on about that bloody angel? You'll have to get out more. Relax. Try yoga- it'll settle your nerves. Read The Little Book of Calm.'*

Maggie can say what she likes but I know what I know. Christy is slipping away from me bit by bit. Only a dot in the distance by now.

'Will you stop,' he says, *'You know I can't stand to see a woman crying. I have to go on a course. It's up in Scotland. I'll be gone two weeks. We'll go to the pictures some night when I come back, that'll put a bit of jizz back into you.'*

This morning Maggie comes in early, all dressed up in her good coat. The kitchen is like a tip-head, smeared marmalade and burnt crumbs and the sink full of last night's dishes. Lighting a cigarette and telling me she's going to her mother's for a while, just for the break. Didn't even know Maggie had a mother. Her eyes on my washed out skirt, the thick blue veins that crawl over my bare shins like roads to nowhere. The angel is back again, standing behind her as clear as day, his wings glittering like bubbles in the sun.

'*It'll be a quiet house now,*' I tell him. '*Maggie gone off to her mother's, Christy in Scotland –just you and me left to make the best of things between us.*'

Maggie stubs out her cigarette and takes out her mobile phone and rings Christy, her eyes sliding away over my shoulder. Knows his number straight off - just like that. She looks different, luminous somehow, like she was lit up from the inside, standing there beside the angel with his bright shadow falling on her face.

Christy is home in half an hour. The two of them with their arms tight around me. Maggie wipes my face with the corner of the tea towel while Christy phones the doctor. He puts down the phone and puts his arms around me again and says that I'm tired out -a good long rest in a hospital would do me the power of good. His voice gentle. His brown eyes shuttered against me.

By the time the doctor comes Christy is still rocking me against his shoulder and Maggie is sitting curled up in a corner of the good leather couch.

Like she was always meant to be there

There's this big, empty space beside her - where the angel used to sit.

DANCING IN THE SNOW

Beezie belonged to my childhood, as much a part of the landscape I grew up in as the stony little fields and the dark conifers that tumbled down the stony shoulder of the mountain. Her lane began at our haggard gate before wheedling its way round by the purple skirts of Knocknashee and past the ruins of Court Abbey where mossy tombstones leaned wearily against the wind. It rambled upwards between deep ditches with tall elms marching shoulder to shoulder on either side until it spilled at last out of the shadows into the muddy yard behind Beezie's house.

The house was like Beezie herself, long and narrow, scowling mistrustfully at the world from beneath heavy, thatched brows. A bare, cobbled yard separated it from the huddle of outhouses that glowered resentfully across at the front door that was turned backside first to the cold bare feet of the Ox Mountains.

Beezie hated everybody. Politicians, priests, nuns, children - especially children. We, in turn, were all half-afraid of her but it didn't stop us making her life a misery. Beezie and ourselves lived in a constant state of war. She'd catch us stealing sour crab apples or chasing the bantam chicks that strayed through the hedge in spite of her best efforts with chicken wire and whin bushes. *'You limbs of the divil,'* Beezie would roar after us with her thin frame shaking with futile anger. *'May bad luck light on the lot of ye.'*

Mother dried our half-frightened tears and comforted us with soft words and current cake.

'*Don't mind Beezie,*' she said, '*the poor woman means ye no harm. You have no call to be bothering her in the first place.*'

Mother told me once, in a rare burst of confidence, how Beezie left her good job in a hotel in Clifden to go home to mind her father when her mother died. The old man lived to be over ninety and by then it was too late for Beezie. The sweetheart she was to have married had grown tired of waiting and went away to London and married a red-haired woman from Galway instead.

Beezie young, with a man in love with her, was beyond our imagining. To us children, she had always been the ancient, ugly witch of the fairytales. She wore faded dresses under dark, cross-over aprons and thick lisle stockings that wrinkled on her thin ankles. Her grey hair, strong as sheep-wire, was bundled into a heavy net and coiled in a bun that was stapled with black hairpins. She never smiled, her eyes snapped at the world from behind steel-rimmed glasses like a pair of bad-tempered cats. She went nowhere but into the town on a Friday to get her pension, sitting bolt upright on an ancient Rudge bicycle in her black coat and faded blue scarf with *Souvenir of Killarney*' printed in the corner. An hour later she was home again with her weeks groceries in a worn hessian bag slung across the handlebars.

She tolerated my father. '*That whelp,*' she called him. Waylaying us on our way up the mountain with her arms folded grimly on her crossover apron. '*Tell that whelp to come up, the roany calf is sick.*' He'd laugh when we told him but he always did her bidding without complaint, even in the depths of winter. Ignoring my mother's soft protest. '*Can't it wait till morning, John?*' No, he said, it couldn't. We were the nearest neighbours. There was nobody else.

A mission came to the parish the year I was twelve. We stood by the kitchen window and watched the missionaries striding up Beezie's lane, dignified and forbidding in Passionist black. Twenty minutes later they were back, scurrying with careful haste through muddy puddles while my father stood in the doorway and watched, his face creased with laughter.

We grew up and went away and discovered the shining, wicked world beyond the Ox Mountains, and came back with suntans and silver studs in our noses, intent on shocking the denizens of the little world we had left behind. Especially Beezie.

But I always brought her something. A bit of lace that I had picked up in some sunny Mediterranean market place, or a gaudy painted jug with misshapen handles. I brought her a butterfly brooch once, woven from silver filigree with' Handmade in Malta' printed on the box. Each offering I made her was a proof of my citizenship of the world. She accepted my gifts with a sniff, and put them on a shelf at the side of the Sacred Heart altar, without comment except once, when she unfolded a black and silver fan, as delicate as a cobweb. *'Wouldn't that be a grand yoke, now, to keep the flies off the butter?'*

My annoyance at her ingratitude amused my father but I was beginning to lose patience with Beezie and her sour sarcasm. It was my mother made me go and see her that last time. I was exhausted, pregnant with my first child, in no mood for the steep trudge up the lane and the grudging welcome that I knew was waiting at the other end. Mother's eyes pleaded. *'She hasn't been all that well lately.'* I sighed; Mother had been saying that about Beezie for years.

'Shut the curse of God door. Do you want to perish the house?'

She eyed me sourly while she unhooked two brown mugs from the dresser.

'You're the full of your apron anyway - you'll end up as fat as your aunt Ellen - God be good to her.'

I flushed. Ready tears threatened to overflow. Beezie plonked the mug of over strong tea gracelessly beside me on the table.

'I have no sweet biscuits in the house-if you're hungry you'll have to do with soda bread.' She didn't bother to wait for my reply but turned her back to me and poked the fire with vicious little jabs of the tongs and I saw with a small stab of angry fear that her hands were shaking.

She followed me to the door as I was leaving.

'Let you be minding yourself now.'

The gentleness in her voice startled me. The ready tears started again and I mopped ineffectually with a crumpled tissue. Beezie snorted.

'When you go down tell that whelp I'm out of turf.' Her voice, sharp with annoyance, followed me across the yard. *'And let you close that curse of God gate.'*

It began to snow as I made my way home down the lane between the frost-bitten fields. The flakes tumbling through the gathering darkness reminded me of my first big dance. The storm, like now, had come stealthily, a few feathery flakes that had grown by nightfall into a blizzard. And I remembered standing shivering in the kitchen in thin blue silk, terrified that the roads would be impassable, praying for a miracle to a seemingly implacable God. There was the sound of foot-steps and the door opening on a blast of icy air. Beezie. Her eyes raking me.

She sniffed. *'That's no dress for a decent girl to be wearing. There's neither a sleeve nor a skirt on it. You might as well be going out in your shift.'* She turned her back to me, looking at my father. *'When I was a lassie, I knew how to dress myself like a Christian. Wasn't I the finest girl in the seven parishes? There was them that said you'd stand in the snow to watch Beezie Brennan dancing.'*

My brother sniggering in the corner started us all off. Beezie turned and walked out, white faced and silent, leaving the door swinging behind her. It was the only time I have ever seen my mother truly angry.

I came down the last bend of the lane into the comforting glow of lamplight shining on wet cobbles. The kitchen wrapped its comfort around me like an old jumper. I met Mother's anxious eyes. *'She's grand,'* I said, *'as contrary as ever.'*

My father found her a week later when he went up to check on the cattle. The doctor said she had been there all night. She was lying under the apple trees as if she was sleeping with the snow drifting round her shoulders like a shawl.

She had willed the farm to a distant cousin none of us had ever seen. She left my father two cows and me a tin box with a picture of mountains on the lid. He brought it to me the week my child was born. I opened it yesterday sitting by the window with my small son beside me, contented in his sleep.

There was a wedding ring and a prayer book-probably her mothers. Five hundred pounds in a used envelope. The butterfly brooch wrapped in yellowed lace. The black and silver fan folded in tissue paper. And at the bottom, under a layer of newspaper grown brown with age -a picture in a narrow frame.

A young girl, slim and beautiful in a white dress that clung and swirled around her like a mist. Her eyes laughing and her dark curls tossing on her shoulders.

I could almost see the young men watching her.

Beezie......... dancing in the snow.

DAISY CHAINS

Bridget was straddling the rock as if it was a horse. The waves slurped greedily at its splayed feet, slurp, slurp, slurp, lipping at the grey ridged stone like a voracious cat.

It was so bloody cold. She locked her arms around her body, her backside numbed into indifference by the spittled damp of the waves and the unyielding stony hollows under her thighs.

Jesus, what a place. What in God's name had ever possessed her? Miles from anywhere. Starving, freezing, only three bloody fags left. She fumbled in a pocket for a cigarette, the match flame a fleeting comfort against the mottled purple of her cupped hands. She inhaled deeply, half-closed her eyes, watching the seaweed clinging like snot to the ridged bleakness of the sands.

The row of houses behind her peeped over prickly, clipped hedges like coy children. Lines of washing flapped in the wind with brisk self-importance. A blue plastic bag hurled towards her; paused and then side-stepped its way gingerly down the rocks towards the beach. A gust of wind caught it and flung it roughly against the nearest wall where it lay panting with futile anger, flapping its defiance against the wind.

Words scuttled around in her head, refusing to be caught. 'Bridget,' she said aloud, 'Bridget, Dixie, Bridget the Midget, Dixie, Darren. Darren and Dixie.'

The words spilled from her mouth in a soupy, meaningless mess.

She threw the cigarette away and laced her fingers into a cradle under her chin and tried to catch the scurrying beetles of her thoughts. Number one - she was pregnant. She was pregnant and Darren had dumped her for that slag Tara Murtagh and Mam would go ballistic. Mam didn't know yet, but Darren did. Oh, Darren knew all right. His eyes, his lovely dangerous eyes that could turn her guts to water sliding past her when they met. Tara and Darren, forehead to forehead, locked together like fighting stags. Jealously rippled through her like a living thing. Jealousy and loss. The secret places of him. Pale hollows under the shadow of his chin, veins as delicate as the markings on the wings of a moth. Darren. *'How are things Bridgie, how's it going?'* His voice ploughing the words into a morass of contemptuous indifference.

'Bridgie.' With his long, beautiful fingers splayed against the whiteness of Tara Murtagh's face.

She'd come straight to Dublin from the bogs of Leitrim, the betraying culchie-flush of freshness on her thirteen-year-old face. They cornered her against the school wall, the swagger of arrogance in their walk. Their eyes flat, one-dimensional. Mocking her. The smell of bus-fumes and stale sweat and the sharper, animal scent of her own terror. They crowded her, smiling lazily through the faint menace of slowly masticating jaws. A huddled, hungry danger.

'This is the new girl-introduce yourselves,' the headmaster ordered them and then turned wearily away.

They obeyed with barely-hidden contempt, slurring the unfamiliar accent as one by one they gave her a roll call of their names. Linda, Tanya, Kylie, Sabrina, Marilyn, Beyoncé, Sharon.

'What's yours, kid?'

Watching her with slow smiles growing in unison on their pinched, feral faces.

'*Dixie,*' she said, '*Dixie.*'

The word, dredged from nowhere, was like a talisman. She said it again. Silently to herself, tasting the brave, strange contours of it against her tongue.

'*Dixie,*' they said. '*Cool. Cool name-Dixie.*' Nudging each other with vicious elbows, '*Dixie. That's like a name you'd give a fuckin' cat.*'

Their laughter was raucous. '*Miaow, Miaow, Nice little pussy, good little pussy.*' Lewdness slackening the sharp angles of their bony little faces.

Then the miracle. The name had somehow stuck and she was Dixie, befriended by Sharon and tolerated by the rest. Big, sweaty Sharon with perspiration stains like half-moons against the sides of the blouse that clung to her massive breasts. Dixie's tormentors circled Sharon warily, all the skinny Lindas and Tanyas and Mandys and Sandras, like jackals in the shadow of a grizzly bear.

'*Fuck them,*' said Sharon easily. '*Fuck the lot of them. Stick with me kid - you'll be alright with me.*'

Sharon lived with her Granny in a small house that clung grimly to the end of a terrace, its frilly curtains lowered over grimy windows like coy eyelashes, as if they were shocked by the obscenity of graffiti on the ribbed steel shutters of the shops across the road.

Sharon's Granny was young - younger than any Granny should be. Her hair was a fuzz of pale orange-tinged blonde. She wore tight leggings and hoop earrings and faded nylon jumpers. She chain-smoked and went to Bingo and the pub every Friday and Saturday night. Her house was a constant tip, heavy with the smell of dogs and stale cigarette smoke and unwashed feet. Everyone called her Imelda, even Sharon. Imelda asked no questions and gave no answers. Offered nothing but strong tea and sugary biscuits and bags of chips on a Friday night. Maybe a Woodbine or a bit of whatever happened to be in the cupboard. Imelda said that after that it was every man for himself and God for us all.

A wave, bigger than the rest, came gliding with smooth menace across the sands, frothing with temper, and crashed against the rock, drenching her to the knees. She cursed, choking back tears of rage and pain and then slid, stiff-legged, to the beach and began to walk back the way she had come. A dog came lolloping towards her, a stick trailing from his mouth. He dropped it at her feet, his head tilted on one side in mute hopefulness. *'Play with me,'* his eyes pleaded, *'play with me.'*

She picked up the stick, smiling, but there was a shout and whistle and as suddenly as he had appeared the dog was gone, russet fur feathering behind him in the wind. She flung the stick from her with vicious strength. It twisted and jack-knifed and fell to the sand a few feet away with a small, defeated plop.

'No Darren,' she shouted despairingly into the wind, *'no Darren, no Sharon.'*

Over and over again, like a skipping rhyme.

Sharon had been her protection. She had felt safe with Sharon. At school discos they holed up in a corner together under the stage, invincible behind a shield of cigarette smoke and Sharon's knowing sniggers, her profane, casual dismissal of what she called the 'fuckin' fellas'. Her sarcasm towards them as savage as her casual, wet-lipped disdain of the girls with their raucous laughter and the desperate, blatant invitation of their angular, half-naked bodies.

But Dixie - Bridget was happy to be invisible behind the harsh flickering of the coloured strobes. Happy and safe in the warm fug of Sharon's protection until the first time she saw Darren and was lost. His eyes seeking her out and his hands pulling her to her feet with the lure of his half-smiling mouth and the black danger of his hair. She remembered the rippled, warm strength of him against her fingers.

'*Stay,*' commanded Darren-his breath warm against her skin. '*Stay with me.*' A command. And she had drifted into the dark shelter of Darren in a haze of incredulous delight and never looked back at Sharon, crouching in the shadows. Never once looked back.

She was freezing, standing at the bus stop. Reading supermarket ads for cut price chickens. '**This week only**!' The pavement was a tangle of crisp packets and used lottery tickets. A few tired pansies slouched half-heartedly against the sides of an ugly cement container.

She frowned, remembering. Granny used to be very fond of pansies. Fat, round-faced things they were, tumbling gleefully out of an old bucket that stood against the pigsty wall. And suddenly she could almost smell the pansies and picture the white emptiness of the narrow road as it hauled itself wearily up past Granny's house and over the steep brow of Cadden's hill and down to the crossroads that led to the Sligo road.

Her mother in the small kitchen, reading a magazine. Granny up to her elbows in flour, mouth pursed in grim disapproval. Mammy lipsticked and pert in too-tight jeans, black rimmed eyes doggedly on her reading and Daddy coming in from the milking, sidling through the uneasy silence and the unspoken hatred and anger of his women. Granny's martyred sighs, the way she swung the big, shining kettle over the fire.

'*Are you hungry son? Will I put a bit of bacon on the pan for you?*' Her mother's high-pitched laugh, the sneering curl of the red mouth and her father's downbent head.

They had met and married in London and came back to Leitrim to live with Granny before Bridget was born. '*Beggars can't be choosers,*' Mammy said. '*Your father is useless –we'll never have our own house. We'll never have anything.*'

But this house, with its long strait-laced body and little windows and shadowed rooms had never suited her mother.

You could never get away from the hate. Even dodging down behind the hayshed and hiding in the shelter of the solid little ditches, it was always there -the hate and the resentment and her mother's thin defiance of Granny.

Granny doted on Bridget. '*Jesus,*' Mammy had screamed once, '*I left London for this. I'd be better off on the streets. I'll go mad.*'

'*Go mad so.*' said Granny, the even menace of the words a soft threat to the child crouched in the corner by the lower room door. '*Go to hell, for you've bought nothing but disgrace and bad luck on my son.*'

Her mother had flung from the room, the mascara running in snail's trails of anger and helplessness down her white, powdered cheeks.

And then Daddy was killed. Faulty brakes on the tractor, they said. The machine rolling down and crushing him and coming to rest at last half-way through the hedge that led into the lower field. Granny found him in the lane lying face down in the mud, his legs twisted and buried beneath him. She thought it was just his old jacket at first, his old green jacket that he wore around the farm, until she came close enough to see the blood and his black curls lifting in the wind. Granny screamed and the sound had come running down the lane on red-hot spindly legs, a small vicious thing that shattered the evening quiet in the dim kitchen. The sound had hit the child like a slap, brought a stinging redness to her face.

The small house was crowded within the hour. '*His black hair,*' Granny wept, '*His lovely black hair.*' He must have smothered, people said wonderingly, each small detail of his dying repeated and lingered over, like a poem, or a prayer.

The funeral was a blur. Her mother's people from Dublin teethered on thin ankles through the muddy little graveyard and talked among each other in strange, flat voices, biting the words off before they were even spoken. She remembered Granny swaying against the black bulk of the priest and the press of the neighbours towards the open grave and the raw wailing of the old woman's voice as she wept for Daddy. '*A mhic O, a mhic o, my lovely, lovely son.*'

There was a cold truce for a while. Small spurts of kindness. Mugs of tea handed silently and grudgingly accepted. The dead man's shadow falling on quiet, evening walls.

Granny's hand on Bridget's head, the hard boniness of old fingers painful against the child's forehead.

'*Poor child, poor unfortunate creature.*' Grief and malice glinting from behind the wire-rimmed glasses. '*What chance is there for you now, and the sort of mother that God left to rear you?*'

Mammy began to smoke more. She took to going to town to the pictures on the bicycle. Her pointed little chin tilted in the face of Granny's cold-faced anger. *'And your man not three months buried.'* The old eyes sliding over her mother's shoulder. *'May God forgive you for I won't.'* Her mother, tender and tawdry in thin cotton, a pale nylon scarf like a drift of mist on her piled -up hair, her mouth a bright, defiant gash in the wanness of her face, swaying out the door, tossing her head like a pony.

Bridget sat in the kitchen, terrified by Granny's rage as the old woman fell to her knees and prayed with viscous piety, the crises-cross of lines on her bent neck like the map of some forsaken country as the Angelus dripped into the quietness and was re-echoed by the bell from the church in the town a few minutes later, like the translucent shadow of a fading rainbow.

Her father faded in Bridget's memory to a dark, ineffectual wraith. She remembered him at the requiem Masses that Granny had celebrated for the repose of his soul when the priest intoned his name like a benison. Her mother defiant and half shame-faced in denim, her hair tinted to the sulky blackness of a dead crow's wing and Granny's shoulders, rigid and righteous under her good, navy coat.

And then the quarrels began. Bridget's mother backed against the kitchen table, her hands claw-like against the ugly, red Formica and Granny, taller somehow, spitting her anger into Mammy's sulky, mutinous face.

'Where are you off to now, which of the bucks are sniffing after you this time? You'll stay at home and mind your child. By God you will.'

Granny's arm raised in threat and her mother with the dull red colour rolling up under her jaw like a welling pain.

'You won't bully me, you evil bitch. You might have had him afraid to draw breath, afraid to touch me, his own wife, but you won't bully me.'

Her mother's hands clenching and unclenching in her distress.

'Rattling your fucking beads in the dark. Don't think I didn't hear you. Praying that your fine son would be too pure to touch his own wife's body. Was that it, you old witch? Did you want him for yourself?'

Granny's hand rising to her throat as her legs plaited and buckled and she collapsed against the chair. And Mammy off down the lane, riding the old bicycle like it was a white horse with a silver bridle.

The next morning was quiet, with the thick quietness of unexploded anger. Her mother, feet propped on a chair, humming softly to herself. *'Be nobody's darling but mine love,'* and Granny putting on her good coat as if it were a burden.

'I'm going into the town. I want to put my affairs in order. I'll get Jodie to come home from Birmingham, so I will. I'll make that decent boy come home and claim his father's land. I'll have no breed of the workhouse walking my man's fields.'

Walking hard-faced out the door, dandruff lying on her shoulders like unmelted snow. And Mammy singing. *'Be nobody's darling but mine love, be honest and faithful and kind.'*

They left three days later, on the seven o'clock bus to Dublin. Her mother waking her with tickles, eyes dancing in the morning whiteness of her face. Nicotine stained finger held warningly against her lips. Clothes all higgledy-piggledy in an unfamiliar suitcase with strong, leather shoulders. Creeping down the stairs in the shared delight of secrecy and escape. The air cool, a loving slap against sleep-warmed skin and the round belly of the creamery can against the byre wall, like some deformed sentinel, its silvery armour a dull gleam against the white-washed stones.

The bus was empty, just like now. They sat at the back, her mother half-asleep, her lashes lying like little, furry smiles against her flushed cheeks.

Oh, but Dublin was big. Dust and noise and trying to dodge the harried thrust of strangers. *'We're home,'* said Mammy, her face soft with pleasure. *'God in heaven, why did I wait so long?'* She dived into Abbey Street like a salmon into familiar waters. Ducking and weaving with careless ease while Bridget scurried, terrified, in her wake. She wanted to wee, tried to press her legs together as she ran. *'Mammy,'* she wailed once but the words were lost in the maelstrom of sound that engulfed them.

They went to Darndale, to her mother's cousin, Mags. Bridget watched her mother glow against the brown Draylon couch in the front room, sitting across from Mags who had brassy, tousled hair and fat hands with gold rings and sagging breasts under a shapeless, tight T-shirt. Heard the ease of venom shared in Mammy's voice. *'Oh, Mags, I could tell you things that would break an angel's heart.'*

They left after a week and rented a flat in Phibsboro and Mammy got a job in a dry-cleaners. But it didn't last and they moved again and Mammy got work to a factory and began to go out with 'the girls' on Friday nights. Wore her skirts shorter and her lipstick glossier and got herself a boyfriend. They never heard from Granny.

Bridget didn't care; she was Dixie by then, strap hanging down O'Connell Street on the number 10 bus, swaying like a circus rider astride a spangled horse. And then Darren. Darren pulling all her dreams together with his gold earring and his black curls and the thick lashes hiding the wicked hunger in his eyes. Howth Head with Darren on a July Saturday, running and running, unfurling herself like a silk banner in the wind.

The bus was empty. The driver was fat, middle-aged, talking over his shoulder to the young conductor who leaned in a lithe, untidy curve against the cab, drawing deeply on an illicit cigarette. She lay back against torn plastic, trying to ignore the insistent tug of wet denim against her legs.

She walked from O'Connell Street, sidestepping push-chairs and stray dogs and litter, drifting along in the slipstream of strangers. Her stomach ached with hunger.

Her jeans felt clammy and uncomfortable, clinging damply between her thighs. People would think she had wet her knickers, and she flushed hotly at the thought.

The house was empty. Mammy was working the late shift, a dirty plate holding the remains of a meal - half a sausage, baked beans, streaks of congealed egg yolk-was still on the kitchen table. The sight made her stomach heave. She made a sandwich from a heel of bread, eating it standing up, leaning against the fridge. The hunger pain eased to a dull ache and she leafed through a magazine as she ate, paused at a picture on the letters page of a small girl squatting on a lawn, frowning with concentration as she tried to make a daisy chain. **'Daisy making daisy chains'** said the coy caption in pink letters.

She found herself smiling, thinking for the first time of a baby. A real baby.

She lit a fag and collapsed into a chair. A little girl. Daisy. Daisy would be nice. They could get a flat, just the two of them, Dixie and Daisy. Or they could go and live with Granny, herself and Daisy with the bunched curls.

The pain flared again and she dragged herself upstairs to the bathroom they shared with the lodger downstairs. There was nobody else around this time of day, the whole house deserted. She ran a bath and. found bath salts left over from Christmas, sprinkled them dreamily in the tepid water and sat on the toilet seat and peeled wet socks from feet that were numbed with cold.

Even Darren would have to melt when he saw their Daisy. He'd have to wait a while though, she had a good bit to go yet - nearly seven months. She touched the flatness of her stomach and smiled.

The cramps were back, stronger this time, making her dizzy. Or a little house maybe. A back garden with a lawn full of daisies. She could buy Daisy's dresses in Guineys. Little pink dresses with matching knickers. Little gold hoops in Daisy's baby ears.

She slipped to the floor, eased the jeans across her hips and over her thighs that were stained and sticky with blood.

She crawled into bed somehow with the cold sweat washing over her. Cold. She was so bloody cold. Darren's eyes glinted at her from the shadowed mirror of the wardrobe. Someone was stabbing her in the gut, slash and slash and slash and she rolled herself into a ball and sobbed for mercy. Don't, she pleaded, it was only a joke, can't you take a joke? It's not Dixie, it's Bridgie. I was only making daisy chains, that's all. Only making daisy chins on the bus, daisy chains for Dixie.

She slipped headlong into the dark.

She drifted up from cold depths, roused by the sound of her mother's voice, high with rage and fright. *'Is it drugs, is it? What's wrong with you? Did you take something, did you, did you? Mother of God, I'll murder you if you took something, bloody murder you.'*

She shivered in the cold wind of her mother's anger.

Weeping and weeping for the agony of her loss.

BURNT UMBER

Divorce, Fiona murmured only this morning as she lay with her scented nakedness draped shamelessly across the tousled bed in her flat, her little teeth nibbling at his cheek, delicate as a cat.

He arrived home earlier than usual, relieved to find the house deserted. A single coffee cup stood upside down on the draining board in the kitchen, a tea-towel neatly folded beside it. There was no sign of his wife and he thought with relief that she probably in the garden. No need to bother her - Rose hated to be disturbed when she was mucking about with her flowers. He stood in the hallway for a minute, admiring as always the floor of polished marble, the gilt-framed pictures on sombre coloured walls.

He climbed the stairs whistling, unbuttoning his jacket as he went.

He hadn't mentioned to Rose that he'd be staying overnight in London, not that she'd have minded if he had. She was just as happy to stay at home. She'd never really enjoyed the wining and dining, the business travelling that was such an intrinsic part of his new successful life. Nobody could ever accuse Barney Madden of being a mean man or a bad husband. He could see that she was as happy as a sand-boy in this lovely house, although sometimes he felt that she took it too much for granted. Rose would have passed out if she knew how much the refurbishment and renovation of the house had cost him. Not that she hadn't earned all of it, the fine house and the big garden and the new car outside the door, he'd be the first to admit that they'd come through some tough times together in the early days and he owed a lot to Rose. Teenage marriages rarely lasted and he felt an odd kind of pride that theirs had survived, was still surviving, longer than most.

Until now he had never so much looked as another woman. But who could blame him? Fiona was young and sophisticated and beautiful and a damned clever woman, she'd shown him a world that, for all his success, he hardly even knew existed. He knew he was lucky to have her. And nobody getting hurt, least of all poor kind, unsuspecting Rose. Still, Barney was nobody's fool. Until this morning the thought of divorce had never even entered his head.

Divorce. A small idea tamped down firmly in a corner of Barney's mind to be taken out and shown the light and then left to sprout into maturity, in Fiona's own good time.

He was startled to find Rose curled up on the wide window ledge of their bedroom, staring at the garden below. He stood in the doorway and looked at her dispassionately, this middle-aged frumpish stranger in sensible tweed skirt and cardigan, with greying hair waved neatly above a wide, lined forehead.

He tossed a travelling bag, obviously new, the shop tags still attached, on the bed and began to pull clothes from the wardrobe.

'*What are you doing up here on your own?*'

'*I was just admiring the garden.*' She smiled at him. '*It's hard work though. Everything seems to go mad at this time of year, especially the weeds.*'

He sighed impatiently, his mind still drowsily full of the memory of Fiona.

'*You should get someone in to help- it's not as if we can't afford it.*'

He glanced at her, frowning as he noted the tired pouched look under her eyes, her cracked nails and reddened hands. Weren't there places nowadays to look after things like that? Beauty shops and nail bars and the like. He'd get Bridget to mention it to her mother as soon as he got home from London.

She caught his glance and reddened and then stood up and moved towards the door, her hands linked defiantly before her.

'*Did you eat? Have you time for something- a sandwich? A cup of tea even?*'

'*I'll grab something on the plane.*' He glanced at his watch.' *I'll have to get a move on. The flight is at six.*'

She sighed and shrugged and went back to her seat by the window. He packed quickly, all his new unfamiliar clothes - dark cashmere sweaters, new underwear, freshly laundered shirts with their shoulders swathed in drifts of tissue paper. He had a personal shopper these days, someone who knew how to dress his new, successful image. Appearances counted for a lot in the world of big business, as he was never tired of telling Rose.

She reached forward and ran a heavy silk tie absently through her fingers.

'*Is Fiona going with you?*'

'*You know damn well she is.*' His voice was heavy with false weariness. '*Fiona is my personal assistant, I'll need her there. This is business, Rose. I'm not doing it for fun.*' He snapped the lid shut on the bag and glanced at himself in the full-length mirror.

'*I mightn't get home until late tomorrow. I'll phone tonight if I have time but the meeting could run late. These guys are serious players.*'

She could see the tightening of his stomach muscles, the almost imperceptible straightening of his shoulders. He brushed her cheek with his lips, shamed and angry by the sudden desolation in her eyes.

'*Bridget knows where I am if you need to get in touch.*'

Bridget, their daughter, her father's partner, colleague, confidante. Bridget, one of Fiona's dearest friends.

'*Bye. I'll bring you back something nice if you're good.*'

After he'd gone she sat again on the bed and thought of Fiona. Lovely, remote Fiona, who was sleeping with her husband. She'd known for of the affair for months, could read the knowledge of his betrayal in the newly buffed sheen of his fingernails, the flicker of distaste behind his eyes when they accidentally touched, the rigidity of his body in her bed.

They'd grown up together, she and Barney, on the sour, stunted acres of neighbouring farms. First love for them both. Barely seventeen, she'd lain beside him in the peppery darkness of the hayshed, shivering at the sly, yearning touch of Barney's thick, powerful fingers side-stepping up her thigh.

'*Marry me Rose and come with me to England. I'll be that lonesome without you.*'

And six months later she'd married him and followed him to Birmingham with nothing but the clothes on her back and the twenty pounds reluctantly peeled from a wad as thick as her wrist by her begrudging father. She spent her wedding night on a ship's deck in the freezing darkness, with the weight of Barney's sleeping form against her shoulder, his breath warm against her skin, freckles spattered like cow's shit on his broad, country face.

England had been good to them. They worked all the hours God sent, she leaving the house in the dead hours before dawn to clean tall office blocks, pubs, factories, and coming home grey- faced with weariness while Barney rose from labourer to foreman on the building sites, finally venturing out on his own, sub-contracting labourers on the lump, making his fortune on the backs of raw faced boys from Sligo and Mayo. But it had been a slow, torturous road from a furnished room in a Birmingham slum to a mock Tudor home in the stockbroker belt.

And then, the siren roar of the Celtic Tiger calling them home.

'I'm sick of England,' Barney said. *'There's fortunes to be made in Ireland now.'*

By the time he told her of his plans, he'd already bought a half-derelict workhouse thirty miles from Dublin. He'd gone over with a few friends to the All-Ireland Final and came back three days later full of the news of his purchase. *'I got it for next to nothing,'* he said, *'the loveliest stone work ever you saw. I have an architect on to it already, when I'm finished with it it'll be a mansion.'*

Rose nodded and smiled, her bent head hiding the desolation in her eyes. She thought of Bridget, their only daughter, a successful banker. She thought of leaving Bridget, of turning her back on her spacious house and lawns, her carefully tended roses, the broad sweep of the river at her garden's end.

'What about Bridget?'

Barney laughed. *'Bridget will be over like a shot. She spends half her free time in Dublin already.'*

Barney was right. Bridget was ecstatic at the idea of moving to chic, happening Ireland. Within three months the house was sold and her husband and daughter were already gone. Rose waited for three further weeks, selling off the furniture, saying goodbye to friends, handing over the keys of her home to an affluent businessman who proposed to turn it into a small hotel.

Barney met her at the airport and drove her straight to the house, impatient as schoolboy, refusing to stop even for a cup of coffee. He swung the car through sagging, rusting gates, parked with a flourish on the overgrown driveway, and flung his arms out as if to embrace the weathered building. The empty windows stared at Rose coldly with blank, unseeing eyes.

'There it is in all its glory.' He hugged her, laughing.

'Your father was right, he always said I'd end up in the workhouse.'

The grey walls turned their backs on her, cradling their secrets in stony, lichen-covered arms.

When the renovations were complete Barney, a new, assertive Barney, hired an interior designer, the daughter of a friend.

'*She knows her job,*' he said, *'I have the money, and I might as well do the thing right while I'm at it.'*

Fiona, a tall self-assured blonde, sat against a backdrop of carved oak panelling, tucking wisps of shining, blonde hair behind ears that winked surreptitiously with the pinprick of diamonds as she made lightening sketches on her pad with swift strokes of a silver pencil. She smiled at Barney as she fanned colour charts in front of a bewildered Rose and expounded her plan to turn the cold, cavernous dormitories into a recreation area of games room, sauna and library. What would they want with a library? The only book they'd ever owned was *Death of an Irish Town,* borrowed by Barney from a mate on the building site, and never returned.

Fiona dismissed Rose's tentative suggestions of almond, magnolia, cream, maybe a nice yellow to brighten up the kitchen.

'We have to think bold here, Mrs Cadden- old gold, burnt umber, sienna sunset.'

Rose stared at the uneven, cut stone walls in bemused silence. The walls stared grimly back, weeping silent, despairing tears of condensation and damp.

Barney, jovial and expansive, smiled at Fiona, frowned warningly at his wife.

'We'll leave it up to you-you're the expert.'

'Thank you, Mr Cadden.'

'Barney it is, girlie, plain Barney Cadden.'

Rose saw the sudden blush, the way the girl leaned forward, her spine rippling under the thin silk of her blouse.

The house was finished for Christmas. Rose moved through elegant, sombre-coloured rooms where old glass -Venetian, early Waterford - gleamed disdainfully against a backdrop of walls painted in burnt umber and deep, brooding blue. The floorboards were stripped and polished to the deep, chestnut patina of Bridget's hair.

Rich swathes of cream velvet fell from the high windows in lush, self-important folds.

Two nights ago she'd overheard Barney talking to Bridget. *'For God's sake will you bring your mother out and buy something decent to put on her back.'* The discreet rustle of money and Bridget's too-bright smile as she suggested that they went shopping together, spent some of Daddy's dosh, her voice high and cajoling, as if she was speaking to an awkward child.

Thirty years before, for Barney's cousin's wedding in a posh country–house hotel, Rose had dressed them both from a second-hand clothes stall in the market. They'd looked, among the elegant, wealthy guests, like shabby gypsies. They slept that night in the back of their old Hillman, huddling together for warmth, and drove home at daybreak, singing rebel songs at the tops of their voices, scraping their last pound together at a roadside café for two Chelsea buns and a shared polystyrene beaker of metallic-tasting tea.

Yesterday a haughty saleswoman eyed disdainfully the silvery stretch marks scribbled across Rose's belly as she swathed her in undergarments that hugged Rose into a firm semblance of an elegant, well-heeled wife. Later, over lunch, Bridget remonstrated lightly with darling, funny, little Mummy for enquiring of the eager, fresh-faced Kerry waiter if he knew a man called Joe O'Leary from Kenmare because Barney worked for years with poor Joe in Birmingham.

Afterwards, in her bedroom, Rose squirmed at the memory and wept tears of helpless, self-pitying rage.

Now, from her high window, she watched Bridget and some of her city friends on the newly flagged terrace below her, as they sat, drinking wine around a table that was lit by fat beeswax candles. Beside them, a stone cherub murmured politely to itself as it dribbled water over a circle of polished stones. Rose leaned longingly towards the light sound of their distant voices. She was in awe of them all, these beautiful strangers. She felt as if she had been abandoned on some strange railway platform, watching helplessly while her husband and daughter whirled away from her, chugging powerfully into a future in which she could have no part.

There was a sudden silence and she heard Bridget's voice, blurry with too much wine. *'Honestly, Mummy is a scream.'* She imitated Rose's flat, midlands, voice with deadly accuracy. *'So you're from Kerry. You wouldn't happen to know a Joe O'Leary from Kenmare by any chance?'* Bridget giggled. *'Fiona thought it was priceless but I almost died of the embarrassment. In Roly's, of all places. I'll never be able to show my face there again.'*

Rose went outside to the patio and stood silently until Bridget, noticing her, looked up startled.

'Mummy, is anything wrong. Has something happened to Daddy?'

A tall redhead sitting across the table leaned over and placed her hand on Rose's bare arm.

'You'd better sit down. Would you like a glass of water?'

Rose ignored the girl .She stared at her daughter coldly.

'I scrubbed floors at six o'clock in the morning to give you the chance of an education that I never had for myself,' she said. *'When you're ready to harrow the field I've ploughed it'll be time enough to tell me what way I should dress and who I should pass the time of day with.'*

She was aware of Bridget's white, shocked face, the sudden embarrassed silence.

'I'm going into the town,' she said. *'Phone your father. Tell him to come home tonight or not to come home at all.'*

In the town she bought a dozen tins of magnolia paint. Two broad brushes. It wasn't going to be easy, ridding the rugged, uneven walls of the signs of his betrayal.

Saffron.

Burnt Umber.

Old Rose.

Wedgwood Blue.

I AM THE SONG, SING ME.

'*Mama,*' I called anxiously,' *are you there, Mama?*'
She was sitting bolt upright on my father's chair,
clutching an old handbag against her chest. Staring at me
with rheumy, dead eyes. Her face had grown thinner -
collapsed into itself like a heap of dead ashes. She wore
bed socks tied with yellow ribbons and unfamiliar clothes
that were too big for her gaunt frame. She had wet
herself again; a trickle of urine still dribbled from the
edge of the chair and the smell of ammonia was heavy in
the frowsy warmth. Suddenly she began to sing in a high,
reedy voice.
'*Come listen to my story, Molly Brawn, for I'm bound for
death or glory, Molly Bawn.*' Over and over and over
again.

I washed the floor and sponged her clean and put
fresh clothes on her yielding, unwieldy body and then
stood by the window watching a blackbird tap-dancing
across the lawn.

After a long time the singing stopped.

The next day I found her a residential home in
Carlow. An ugly, functional building whose grey bricks
might have once looked aesthetic and elegant on some
architect's drawings but were now streaked and mottled,
like stains of sweat on a fat woman's blouse. Mama had
never been in Carlow, nor knew anyone from that place.
It made no difference - Carlow or Calcutta, they were all
the same to her now.

The nurses shooed me away with kindly, brisk impatience. When I saw her again she was sitting by the window, wearing a new blue nightdress that barely reached to her knees. Underneath it her legs were dappled with purple, the skin stretched over the knotted calves so tightly that it shone. Silvery threads of spittle criss-crossed her chin, like fishing lines glinting in the sun.

'Mama? Mother?'

Her hand lay flaccid and unresponsive under mine, as cold and clammy as dead chicken skin. She was humming again, an unintelligible sound like a wasp trapped behind a windowpane. After a minute she pushed my hand away and examined her own grubby fingernails with minute attention, like a bored teenager at a bus stop.

I sat on a low stool in the kitchen watching Mama baking bread. I must have been about six. There were three brown freckles on her smooth arms, just below the elbow, like a little face that dimpled and smiled at the stretching and folding of her skin.

Her eyes danced at me. **'Will we make a pancake for Dada's supper?'**

I fetched the big yellow bowl from the dresser and she tossed in eggs, flour, milk, sugar, a pinch of salt, her hand guiding my smaller one as I whisked and stirred.

She was singing. **'Come listen to my story Molly Bawn, for I'm bound for death or glory Molly Bawn.'**

Her voice was high and sweet, like a blackbird after rain.

We set the table with the blue and white mugs and she stacked the pancakes on a plate with a gold rim and, beside them, three lemons with their yellow nipples upended in a glass bowl.

'Molly made them her own self,' she *told my father when he came in from the milking.*

'Our Molly Bawn made the pancakes for your supper.'

I sat and watched him eat with my striped blue and white dress fanned around me, hugging my scabby brown knees in delight.

The tired–faced professionals reassure me that she is happy now in the grey world she lives in. Her brain is dying, they tell me, and her mind can no longer process emotions of loneliness and betrayal and pain. They are kind to her-those carers who coax her and coo over her as if she was a child, running tender fingers along the ugly purple bruises on her arms. She loses her balance a lot lately, they tell me, as they scold fondly, wagging admonishing fingers in her unheeding face.

'You're a naughty, naughty, girl Annie, you must have been pinching the brandy again.' We smile together at their little joke and I wish I could slap their smug, sunny faces and wrap her safely in my arms and run with her, back and back and back to the place where she was Mama and we made pancakes for the supper and I was Molly Bawn.

I was twelve the Summer Liam broke my heart. She wiped my tear-stained face with a corner of her apron and folded away her knitting.

'My eyes are worn out counting these stitches,' *she said,* **'We'll go into the town to the pictures. Let your father get his own tea - it won't kill him for once.'**

She brushed and looped my hair in clasps that were the shape of butterflies with folded wings and tied a pale silk scarf patterned with roses under her chin while Dada sulked and watched us with flat, resentful eyes.

She bought me a packet of toffees in Lynch's shop and then, as an afterthought, an apple. We flew down the hill into the town, freewheeling past the school and the old haunted flax-mill with Mama singing and our bicycle wheels whirring like grasshoppers in the sun.

I sat entranced in the foetid Saturday evening darkness-heedless of fumblings and soft groans and sighs that thickened the air around me. She stirred uneasily beside me and once I caught her anxious, sideways glance, but I was blind and deaf to everything but the fly- mottled screen and the beautiful, laughing face of the saloon dancer called the Scarlet Angel.

I galloped home across the starlit prairie and down past Middletown crossroads sitting tall in the saddle of my second-hand bike with my head flung back and my silver spurs and scarlet satin dress dappled with moonlight. Then my wheel struck a stone and I sailed across the handlebars into Reilly's lower field. She teethered on the ditch above me, ungainly in her good Summer sandals, anxiously calling my name.

'**Molly? Are you all right, Molly Bawn?**'

She clambered down and knelt and gathered me in her arms where we clung together, shaking with smothered laughter.

'**That horse**,' *she said gravely,* '**he's the devil if you don't watch him at the ditches.**'

She bent and wiped the spattered cow's shit from my legs with her good silk scarf and tossed it carelessly away. It caught and fluttered on a bush and hung like a flag of glory, with its painted roses faded to silver in the moonlight, long after we were gone.

'*No harm done,*' she said, '*we won't mention it to your father.*'

I've lost count of the journeys I've made to Carlow, all the early morning starts from the city with half the world still asleep. I've come to dread the familiar tedium of deserted city streets and drowsy suburbs melting into fields that are shawled with mist as juggernauts come thundering towards me out of the darkness, shouldering me from their path.

It's raining now, a peevish, bad-tempered mist that even in the warmth of the car, seems to chill me to the bone. I pull into an early morning café and drink lukewarm coffee and consider the futility of my sacrifice. Mama doesn't even know me anymore. My hand that she clutches with such surprising strength could be anyone's hand. The snatches of songs she sings for me are meaningless, mangled sounds that fall from her mouth in an unintelligible mess. The last time I saw her she smelled of shit and disinfectant. Her eyes were flat, shutting me out from the workings of what is left of her mind. I sat for two hours, facing her, watching the clock on the wall as it ticked primly, chopping the remains of her life into precise little slivers of time. She ignored me until I got up to leave and then she clutched piteously at my arm with her eyes glossy with tears.

'*Bring me home Josie for the love of God bring me home.*'

I detached her fingers gently from the delicate cashmere of my cardigan.

'*I'm Molly, Mama, your daughter, Molly.*'

A nurse came and wrestled her hand away and she clawed ineffectually at the woman's face. As I walked away she began to wail with the high, bewildered anger of a thwarted child.

When I go outside I find that the rain has stopped, and a watery sun smiles tentatively from behind wisps of cloud as I turn the car for home. I imagine the delighted relief on my husband's face and the uncomplicated warmth of the children's welcome. They hate these 'Granny days' as they call them, dreading coming home to a cold, empty house, struggling with homework while my husband, Don, scolds and shouts as he wrestles with the microwave.

There was the dance in Gowna hall the Summer I was sixteen. Everyone else was going-I told my father. Everyone but me. I'd have to stay at home; I hadn't a stitch to wear. **'Haven't you the house full of clothes?'** *he demanded.* **'Didn't your Aunt Bridie bring home armfuls and armfuls of lovely dresses from America last summer? The best of dresses. You wouldn't get dresses like that in O'Connell Street in Dublin.'**

He knelt beside the big tin trunk under the window and dragged out beaded velvets and yellowing lace and wide skirted flounces buoyed up by stiff petticoats.

'Look at that,' *he said,* **'silks and satins that's fit for a queen. You'll be the belle of the ball so you will. The belle of the ball.'**

She told my father that I needed new school shoes -the old ones were worn to the road. On Tuesday we went to Cavan on Ned Maguire's bus. She carried her money in a leather purse pinned to the inside of her coat with a safety pin. In Maurice Brady's shop she called me to admire dowdy, pleated, plaid skirts and twin sets with little pearly buttons, and laughed aloud at the sight of my stricken face, teasing me with her young-girl eyes.

We bought a tee shirt with black and silver stripes. A mini skirt in singing scarlet. Shiny white boots. Delicate, lacy tights. **'Would you look at the price of them tights,'** *she demanded of the shop girl, counting out half-crowns on the counter.* **'Three pounds of good money for a wisp.'** *She hid the parcels in her shopping bag, under a head of cabbage as we walked down Bridge Street with linked fingers, smiling our shared delight.*

I dressed for the dance in a blue, beaded dress that smelled of wilting roses.

'Lord,' *said my father,* **'but you'd look gorgeous, if it wasn't for them boots. Could you not wear your new shoes? You look a sight in that lovely dress with them boots?'**

She took my arm and hurried me out the door.

'I'll walk down with you,' *she said,* **'it's too dark for you to be out on your own.'**

In Cullen's hayshed she took the parcel from under her coat.

'Hurry now, *she said,* **'before someone sees the light and thinks it's old Cullen's ghost.'**

She smoothed the scarlet skirt over my hips with anxious hands, her eyes starry in the half darkness.

'Aren't you the beauty,' *she said.* **'You'll knock the sight out of the young men's eyes.'**

She gathered the blue dress up and hid it under her coat.

'I'll leave the back door on the latch for you. Try not to waken your father.'

The sun is shining bravely as I stop at a gateway of a house with a freshly -mown lawn where a woman sits on a plastic chair, reading. A small child, naked except for a hat, crouches under a weeping willow, playing with a toy bucket full of water. The woman looks up, startled, and half rises as I wave and then reverse carefully into her gateway and wait for a break in the traffic.

Luke Kelly is belting it out on the radio *'Oh, Oh, Glorio, I am the Lord's disciple.'* he sings lustily and I pull out into the slipstream of a passing lorry and sing along with Luke and watch the signposts flash past.

This next one, white on a dark green background, says **'CARLOW - 17 MILES.'**

CAT'S EYES

Most people would probably think that a coffee shop right in the centre of a busy city street is far too public to be a romantic rendezvous. But despite the crowds, the noise, the ceaseless comings and goings, this is our special place, John's and mine. We've spent enough time here over the years, goodness knows, to entitle us to claim some sort of ownership. Even the waitresses recognise that we have our own special table. This is where we had our very first date. Twenty-four years ago now, and we've been together ever since. Sometimes I almost resent the intrusion of other people. It means nothing to the bloated businessman and tired housewives and bewildered-looking tourists surrounding us, it's just another coffee shop they have wandered into by chance.

Even long before I met John this room always seemed like a refuge to me, a place where I could feel safe, cradled and sheltered by the high mirrored walls, even on a freezing day like this when the sky is dark with threatened snow. It's not surprising that the place is so popular-the building itself is a national landmark. It's in all the tourist brochures and according to them the cafe is *'world-renowned'* for its coffee and wonderful pastries, not to mention the ghosts of long-dead poets and writers who haunt it after dark.

My parents were elderly when I was born. I was their only child. Yet my mother made it clear after my father's death that she would prefer to live alone which is why, at the age of eighteen, I moved to Dublin and rented a damp high ceilinged bed-sitter in Rathmines that, in all the years I lived there, I could never call home. I rarely went home again except for brief visits at Christmas and Summer. My mother had her life of golf and knitting circles, and I had mine.

I found a job in a solicitor's office and for the next fifteen years I spent my days typing endless documents for Mr Stuart Littleton, a taciturn, dour-faced man who rarely spoke of anything but business. On the rare occasions we met my mother nagged me to find something more suitable to my qualifications, by which she meant better wages and the chance to find a husband. But I stayed with Mr Littleton, the pay was adequate and it suited me to be left to my own devices. I was used to being alone, even as a child, existing contentedly on the periphery of other people's lives.

A happy accident, I call our first meeting, although John always said it was fate that brought us together. Both of us running for a bus to escape the sudden onslaught of a Summer downpour and colliding like two meteorites on the edge of the pavement. Standing, smiling and winded with the rain pouring down our faces while the bus trundled uncaringly over the canal bridge and out of sight. He touched my cheek with his fingers. Checking for broken bones, he said, his voice bright with laughter. We ended up walking into town together, the rain softening to mist while we talked with the easy familiarity of old and trusted friends. Somewhere around Stephen's Green our palms had met and clasped, and we walked down Grafton Street with our entwined fingers swinging between us, like a pair of teenagers in love.

We sat here for hours, at this very same corner table, just talking, while tired-faced waitress patiently filled and refilled our cups. A long time later we strolled up Rathmines Road in the dusk with the big green dome of the church glimmering like a hovering space ship and the rain darkening and sleeking John's hair to silk.

The next time we came here the sun was shining through the skylight of coloured glass. John looked up, smiling, and promised that we would have a window in the roof of our house like it-so that every morning it would be like waking up under a rainbow.

Nothing ever seems to change here. The same middle-aged waitresses still wear sensible black skirts under starched, frilly aprons. The seats are still upholstered in leather cracked with age. The blue and white cups are piled high on old-fashioned wooden counters. It is such a comfort to me that everything still looks exactly the same. The skylight still filters the light on the polished floors like skeins of coloured silk. There is that same wonderful smell of cinnamon and freshly ground coffee and the waitresses still scurry past like flustered magpies in their lacy caps and spotless buttoned-up blouses and John is still sitting opposite me in our special, secluded corner, his dark eyes dancing, full of laughter.

I like sitting here quietly with John, not speaking, watching the people around me and stealing glances at his loved, familiar face. Sometimes I'm afraid that if I close my eyes he will have disappeared altogether. But that's being silly. He's always there- smiling that slow, lazy smile that I fell in love with the very first time I saw him .We hardly notice the other customers –we are so wrapped up in our own private little world. Maybe that's why I was so annoyed just now with the sad, fat, tired-looking woman with pudgy ankles and over-flowing shopping bags who came and set her tray right in the middle of our table her rain-spattered glasses on the corner of her scarf. Such a shabby looking creature in her ugly, grey anorak and yellowy, washed-out blouse.

We ignored her and she ignored us in turn as she poured tea and picked at a cherry bun with pink and white icing. I frowned at such lack of good manners but the woman only settled herself more comfortably in her chair.

'*Shocking weather we're having,*' she said and I nodded and then turned deliberately away and offered John more coffee, pressing him to have just one more chocolate éclair. He smiled and shook his head, his shadowed face almost invisible against the smoke-blackened leather.

'*This is a table for two,*' I said, just loudly enough for a passing waitress to hear. '*It's far too crowded for three people.*'

John is always teasing me about my habit of speaking my thoughts aloud. It's our private joke- he says I lived alone for too long. It's a good thing, he said, that he had rescued me when he did. Millie, his sister, just gets angry and turns on me, tight-lipped with fury.

'*For goodness sake stop talking to yourself. Helen, people are watching.*'

As if I care. But sometimes she gets so annoyed that she refuses to speak to me for days. The woman stared, open-mouthed and then turned her head away and gathered her bags together and stood up so abruptly that she knocked over the sugar bowl in her haste.

Of course none of them wanted us to marry. Not John's family and certainly not my mother. It was too soon, they all said. We should wait until we were certain.

We were both too long single, too set in our ways. '*It isn't easy, sharing someone else's life,*' my mother warned me sternly, '*you only know him a few weeks-how can you be sure?*'

I ignored the incredulous anger in her eyes when I told her we had found our house and set the date for the wedding. I was making a big mistake, she said, she would have no part in it. She stood by the open door, white faced with anger and to give me courage I touched the soft silk of the green silk scarf that was wound around my throat and fastened with a silver pin. My lucky green scarf, my talisman that John bought it for me because it matched my eyes. Emerald eyes, he called them. Beautiful, sleepy, emerald cat's eyes .We said goodbye and John just helped me on with my coat and unwound the scarf and tied it tenderly under my chin as if I was a beloved child rather than his soon-to-be wife.

We never did find our house with a coloured skylight and in the end we settled for a terraced cottage facing the canal. We had so much fun turning that dark neglected little building into a home. And bit by bit the overgrown wilderness beyond the back door became a flower filled garden waiting for the children that never came. We minded about the children for a long time and then it wasn't important any more. It was more than enough happiness for us that we had each other. And when we were parted, for however brief a time, I wore my green scarf, my charm that never lost its power until the night I stood by the window for hours and still he didn't come home and I knew something terrible had happened. The fear drove me from room to room like a mad thing, my green scarf knotted between my fingers like a rosary and then, when I could bear the waiting no longer, the doorbell finally rang and it seemed as if all the waiting had gathered in a cold lump against my heart. I knew. Even before I saw the young Guard with his long, girlish eyelashes and the torch shining uselessly in his gloved hands.

'*Accident*,' he said. '*There's been an accident*.' In the distance I heard someone scream and for a minute the world turned black around me as strangers, neighbours we barely knew, came running from their lighted doorways, their face soft with pity and distress and a woman in a flowered apron put her arms around me and held me against her shoulder in the rainy dark.

The police car smelled of vomit and stale clothes. A young girl in uniform sat beside me and held my hand folded tightly between her own. I can never forget the nightmare of that journey nor the young woman's voice. She had such a lovely, lilting voice.

I remember staring out the window at shops blurring past in the darkness and Christmas lights that danced across the wet pavements like drowning rainbows. Reindeer and stars and coloured lanterns and bells strung across the city streets tossing and swaying like flowers in a summer storm.

Millie was waiting for me inside the wide hospital doors that had skeins of tinsel wound around the handles. She was red-eyed, as if she'd been crying. She tried to catch me in her arms as I blundered past, pushing her from my path. I needed none of them, not the policeman or the doctors or Millie. Only John. He lay white-faced and bandaged with the tubes snaking around his bed like living things. I sat beside him all night and prayed and listened to the blip, blip, blip of machines as they measured out the minutes of his life. I ignored the doctors with their tired faces and Millie in her grey coat while John and I clung together in all that alien brightness and fought the demons of the dark.

That's all over now, all the heartache and worry. We are back again, safe in our own special place and John is smiling at me as I wipe the tears from my eyes and here's Millie again in her grey coat. Always in grey.

'There you are Helen,' she says. *'Silly girl, running off like that. I was getting quite worried about you.'*

Millie's voice is high and bright, as if she was speaking to a child. Her coat is unbuttoned and her hair is dishevelled, bundled under a woollen cap. People are turning around to watch as she beckons to the waitress and they whisper together, watching me slyly from the corners of their eyes.

The girl at the till smiles at Millie like a conspirator.

'Not again,' she says to Millie, and sighs. *'That must be the third time this month.'* She shakes her head and they both turn to look at me as if I was a naughty little girl and not a grown woman, John's wife.

Millie' face is folded in lines of concentration as she painstakingly counts out money from her purse and accepts her change. In the mirrored wall behind the till I can see her reflection, her wind reddened cheeks and untidy hair. A tall, elderly woman stands patiently behind her, slump shouldered, her face folded in lines of sadness. The woman is weeping, she wrings her hands together and wipes the snails-trails of tears from her cheeks with a green silk scarf. She looks familiar somehow and I narrow my eyes, my green cat's eyes, staring at her, trying to remember. The woman's face looks back at me, her eyes sunken and dark with unshed tears. Light bounces from polished table tops and dim, mirrored walls.

But I never see John's face in the mirror any more.

THE DARK SIDE OF THE MOON

'All right now darling? Warm enough?'

Mother strokes the arm of my wheelchair as if it was a favourite pet before she patters away like an elegant little White Rabbit, admonishing herself for being late again - silly, silly girl. Just look at the time.

I sit by the window, waiting, watching the clear November sunlight grow sharper with the cold, outraged beauty of the first frost.

I am thirty-six years old. I have never walked or spoken or even smiled in any recognisable manner. There were great hopes for me once - but they came to nothing in the end. People don't speak to me directly, they carry on their bright, inane conversations with the air above my head.

Yet my mind is normal, as far as I can tell. I know a beautiful woman when I see one, or a good painting, or a stylish sports car. I can read the night sky. I like the scent of freshly–cut grass, cigar smoke, flowers after rain. I am mesmerised by the sight of snow falling through the branches of bare winter trees. I know that physical ugliness, even my own, repels me. I can't do much about any of those things. I can't do much of anything-except wait to be fed and dressed and moved from A to B and back again.

I've become very good at waiting.

In another hour Mother will be playing her weekly round of golf with her dearest friend, Monica. (*Honestly, Monica, there's no justice in the world. Thank God I have my*

Tuesdays) -and afterwards they will lunch together in that Italian place on Chapel Row, where the ciabetta is as good as anything you can get in Naples. Monica will commiserate sweetly while Mother sighs soft, brave sighs until, after their third gin and tonic, they begin to see the funny side and laugh together with rich flutiness, like drunken blackbirds, as they share (just for Tuesdays) the crown of Mother's martyrdom.

Well, dearest, darling Mother-have I got news for you? Sister James - you remember Sister James Mother, so much mutual admiration, has just popped in and performed a beautifully rehearsed double-take at the sight of me before she tosses her bombshell into my misshapen lap.

'What on earth are you doing here, Philip? Didn't they tell you that your Tuesdays have been cancelled?' She sighs.

'I'd better tell Julia or Tillie you're here - you'll probably need feeding.'

And Sister James struts away in her cheerful red blouse, all starch and padded Playtex, like an affronted robin.

So make the most of lunch, Mother because it seems you've been right all along. It ain't right and it ain't fair. But that's the way it is. Like the song says - the band has stopped playing, the dancers are leaving, and the party is finally over.

Now where's the justice in that?

The sour, acrid smell of Julia and Tillie whoosh into the room before them, pungent as a smothered fart.

'Philip, pet, we forgot all about you.' Rich chuckles running through Tillie's voice like melted butter. Even her glance is moist with pity.

'*Poor devil -you must be falling off your feet with the hunger.*'
She brightens.

'*There's a bit of custard left in the kitchen, I'll get Julia to spoon it into you.*'

'*I don't want any bloody fucking custard.*'

Julia opens the window and tosses out the stub of her cigarette and a blast of November air rushes in and transforms our breaths into pale, ectoplasmic ghosts. I shiver and she smiles vaguely in my direction.

'*It can't be helped, pet. If tight -arse smells the smoke there'll be murder.*'

'*I'm fucking freezing to death here.*'

'*What's wrong with you now, love?*'

Julia's nostrils are full of tiny hairs, delicate as the legs of flies. A silver tuft sprouts enquiringly from a mole on her left cheek, like a worm coming up for air.

She pats my head absently with hands that are red and swollen like slices of raw liver and frowns.

'*I know, pet. You're starving. Here's Tillie now with your custard.*'

The custard crouches sulkily on a thick plate, red jelly bleeding around its gloopy edges. A fly sits on the plate's rim and rubs thread -like legs together in anticipation of the feast. Tillie's breasts swing sadly against my face as she shoos him away and deftly scrapes the spilled custard from my chin.

There are pale half -moons of dried sweat on the underarms of her white cardigan.

'*I said I don't want any fucking custard.*'

'*I haven't all day - you're not supposed to be here at all according to her ladyship.*'

'*Her ladyship can kiss my arse.*'

'*Less of the blarney now . Eat up for Tillie like a good boy.*'

Her eyes are suddenly colder - coded with hidden warnings.

Mother would be horrified at the vulgarity of my language (if she could understand a word I was saying), because after all, despite everything, we are still the Bennetts. Grandfather Bennett was a pillar of rectitude in the community. After Father left, before I grew too big and ungainly for them to manage, Grandfather and mother took care of me themselves. It's a small town, as Grandfather always reminded us. Some things are best keep private.

Mother assures everybody that I am her dearest treasure, while managing to convey- without using so many words- that I am also her cross, her gladly-shouldered burden, her claim to sainthood in this world and the next.

'*My first and my last - I didn't dare have any more children after poor Philip.*'

Whispered confidingly to her closest friends as she sips her after-dinner brandy with such a delicate little shudder of those fragile, brave shoulders.

But Mother never confides to even her closest friends that darling daddy, the other half of the production team that fell down on the flawed masterpiece of their only son, took one disgusted look at me and fucked off to New Zealand and never came home again. That's our little secret, Mother's and mine. Grandfather knew, of course- but he's dead and Father doesn't count - he's been on the other side of the world for thirty-five years and has probably forgotten all about me by now.

So it was fortunate that Grandfather, mindful of the injustice of the blow dealt to Mother and to the Bennett good name, provided for her so handsomely in his will, leaving her a generous annuity and his spacious, gracious home. And he didn't forget me, his only grandchild, his sole living male heir, his hostage to fortune.

He left me his telescope.

His contempt.

His love of graceful, beautiful things.

I wasn't allowed to attend the funeral. Mother felt it would be too stressful all round. The church was too small to accommodate a wheelchair and my vocal chords can be somewhat unruly. They have been known to make loud, embarrassing noises of their own violation at the most inappropriate moments. Mother didn't mention this but even I realised that it was not at all the sort of occurrence to interrupt the muffled weeping and the somewhat ragged chorus of *Abide with Me*.

When Grandfather's obituary appeared in the local newspaper she read it aloud to me, her voice shivering with tears. She sat beside me so brave and beautiful in her mourning black, and held my hand while she read. Devoted husband, loving father, adored and adoring grandfather. Sadly missed by his many friends. May his gentle soul rest in peace. *(Such a pity, darling. You two could have been such friends. Everyone simply adored Father.)*

Grandfather was barely six months dead when the Respite Centre opened and took me off Mother's hands for one whole day every week. The answer to all our prayers. Since then I've been hardly any trouble at all. The cleaning woman feeds me, Mother puts me to bed, and until now, I've had my Tuesdays.

Who's a lucky boy then?

Mother will be on her fourth gin by now *(Honestly, Monica, I don't know how I keep going)*, and will have become so bitter that by the time we get home she'll be incandescent with rage at the enormity of her misfortune. She'll decide on an early bedtime for me in Grandfather's room that has been specially adapted to my requirements and undress me herself with just the right amount of gentle viciousness in her pretty, pink-tipped hands. And then stand in the doorway and switch the light off with smiling deliberation.

'Good night Philip.'

'Sod you, Mother dearest.'

Grandfather's telescope is mounted on a table beside my bed, angled so that on bright nights I can turn my head to the window and watch the sky. I remember nights when I was younger and the medical men still held out some hope, nights when he sat by my bedside, murmuring to himself the strange and wonderful names of the mountains and the oceans of the moon. Oceanus Procellarum, Mare Ibrium, Mare Crisium. The starburst of Tycho Copernicus. I remember them still. And I remember too the sound of his deep, beautiful voice as he wondered aloud about the unknown darkness on the other side.

On a bright night with no rain, I am the Man in the Moon.

Tillie scrapes the last of the custard from my chin and spins my chair towards the window.

'All finished now, pet. You can look out at the nice garden.'

I lie slumped with my face (twisted, plug-ugly, I know, I know,) angled so that the edge of the chair cuts viciously against my chin and I writhe with futile anger and stare at the high pebble dashed wall that cuts me off with uncaring spite from the sun.

Tillie reads aloud from the magazine she is holding. *'The importance of foreplay.'* She moves closer to Julia and whispers behind her cupped hand and Julia leans forward eagerly, her fat fingers folded like skeins of sausages in her lap and snorts, her face suffused with scandalised laughter.

'Foreplay my arse.'

The pain in my jaw is becoming unbearable and I moan with agony until they exchange warning glances, frowning and folding their mouths into reluctant silence. Julia shrugs and closes the magazine.

'Don't mind poor Philip, he hasn't a clue, have you pet?'

She drinks her tea in noisy slurps.

'I'm choking here, you stupid bitches.'

'Poor fellow, were you slipping?' I can feel the revulsion through their roughly biting fingers as they grab me in unison under the armpits, propping me upright again like an ungainly puppet.

In another minute they are once again immersed in their second-hand titillation and I close my eyes against the sight and return to my waiting.

Sunlight trickles reluctantly over the grey wall. I drift into sleep and wake again at the sound of Tillie and Julia leaving. They remind each other that they are supposed to clock off at three. It's already ten past. They have homes to go to, children to feed, soap operas to watch. Tillie and Julia are working women, not unpaid babysitters. The door clicks shut behind them. The round yellow clock on the opposite wall drips the minutes reluctantly into the quietness and stares at me with its implacable Chinaman's face. I close my eyes again and fill my mind with puerile lists of the things I love - books songs stars on a dark night the names of pubs on the main street in Ardee Bizet football on telly Emmy Lou Harris the swirl of brandy in a glass Paul Durkin the teasing twirl of a woman's dress the smell of rain the downy curve of Marianne's cheek, the roundness of her hips in a white dress the glint of the name badge on her breast.

Building futile bulwarks against the desolation of Tuesdays in my mind.

The door swings open again and my Marianne glides through, her strong, beautiful hands guiding Molly in her wheelchair. Marianne turns the wheelchair towards me and wags an admonishing finger in my face.

'*No funny business now Philip, I know all about you and your way with the girls.*'

Her mouth curves but only the front of her eyes smile and then slide away over my shoulder as Molly pulls at my sleeve, her little piggy eyes squinting with delight.

'*Marianne bing Molly to moosic.*'

My flesh crawls at the sound of the bright gold curves of Marianne's name being masticated to a nasal mulch by the workings of Molly's slack, spit-shiny lips.

'*I brought her to a concert last night,*' Marianne sighs. '*Poor little thing loved it, didn't you pet?*'

Molly leans closer. '*Tiss Molly.*'

The bile rises in my throat as I watch the snail's trails of saliva glinting on her chin. In desperation I snarl and bare my teeth and Molly squeals like an enraged pig, flinging her arms around my neck.

Marianne says mildly '*Mind Philip's sweater, darling,*' and leans across me and folds Molly's fat, distorted fingers tenderly in her own slender palms. She cradles the ugly, snot-streaked face tenderly against the curve of her breast. Her eyes accuse me but I stare defiantly back.

Quasimodo and Esmeralda, Beauty and the Beast.

Why not why not why not why not?

Mother arrives punctually at four o'clock, kitten heels tapping a staccato warning to herald her coming. She rushes into the room in a flurry of smiles and apologetic pouts, her high, girlish voice crackling at the edges with the gaiety of her laughter as she swoops and dutifully kisses the air above my head.

'Hello people. How's my handsome boy then? How's Mummy's sweetheart?'

Her smile encompasses all of us, me, Marianne, Molly (*I see you're flirting with Molly again, you sly old Romeo*), and my bray of disgusted fury is airily interpreted as delighted laughter at her wit.

Mother accepts the news of our cancelled Tuesdays with laughing courage. (*Cutbacks- of course I understand. Really, governments are so uncaring. But it's very unjust to poor Philip-he does so love it here- I can't imagine how he'll manage without his Tuesdays*).

We say goodbye with dimpled smiles and sighs of bewildered gratitude and I wave to my beautiful, sexy, golden Marianne as Mother stows me away deftly in the expensive car that she drives with such careless confidence.

'Far too big for a little person like me, but poor Philip, you know- the chair...'

Rough justice Mother. But necessary. You've read the papers like the rest of us. The Government isn't a bottomless pit. It all costs money, what with motorways and tearaways and joy riders and fact –finding junkets for the boys. Their need is so much greater than ours. Of course, the golf will probably have to go, and the Italian lunches -but then you can't have everything.

We swing down the driveway and the back of Mother's neck is taut with fury. Her eyes in the mirror are brilliant with rage, like shards of glass in an empty window. She clenches her small fist and strikes the dashboard with compacted fury.

'*The unfeeling bureaucratic bastards. It's so unjust. They were all I had- my Tuesdays. What the bloody fucking hell am I going to do with him now?*'

Language Mother, please. Remember, despite everything, we are still the Bennetts.

The car sweeps through the gateway as the rain begins and the wipers go tumble and swish, tumble and swish to the terrifying, hopeless sound of Mother's weeping.

And I wonder what life will be like for me now - on the dark side of the moon?

DISCO QUEEN

'*Can I go to Dizzies Friday night?*'
'*No.*'
'*Please Ma.*'
'*No.*'
'*That's not fair, everyone else is going.*'
'*I don't care if the Pope of Rome is going - you're staying at home. You're still only fourteen, your father wouldn't hear of it.*'
'*I don't care what he says. I'm going anyway.*'
'*Lisa!*'

But Lisa was already gone, the front door slamming so hard behind her that the cups chattered and danced together on the kitchen table. Her mother dropped her head into her hands and tried to knead the ache from her forehead with the tips of her fingers. Kids. There soon wouldn't be a door in the house left on its hinges. Was it only last year that Lisa was obsessed with roller blades and Barbie dolls? Now it was black nail varnish and nose rings and threats of tattoos on the still rounded childish curves of Lisa's arms. And the young lad, the one they met in the shopping centre only yesterday as she was coming out of Tesco with Lisa beside her scarlet-faced, ducking her head like a skittish pony.

He smiled at them both, blue eyes dancing, raising a hand in careless greeting as he passed.

'*Who's that?*' she asked, but Lisa just mumbled, '*Hiya Paul - c'mon Ma,*' tugging at her mother's arm like an insistent toddler. She turned and watched as he walked away in his tight jeans and silver studded brows and tooled leather boots, his dark hair spilling on his shoulders. An Apache warrior, beautiful and dangerous, utterly alien to her safe, familiar world.

She sighed now and poured more coffee and watched with faint annoyance as the pale winter sunlight fingered the smudges on worktops and walls. Maybe they were too protective of Lisa, herself and Joe. After all, most of the child's schoolmates were out every weekend, some of them had boyfriends since they were eleven or twelve years old. Madge from next door thought they were mad. Madge was a Dub from Ballyfermot. She had six daughters.

'Jaysus, Sheila, what different is she from the rest? Haven't they all to go out and face the world sometime?'

But Sheila and Joe - they came from a different world. Country people from Mayo. Not a wet week in Dublin either of them when they met in the Ierne on a Sunday night. Joe whirling her through a sea of silent city streets faces to the strains of an old time waltz. Walked her home through unfamiliar city streets while she hobbled in too-tight shoes, clinging to his arm. She sometimes thought that they had been clinging together for survival ever since.

Madge, with her big heart and her fags and her kids that had babysat each other every Saturday night since the oldest was ten, was from another world. But Madge was right, Lisa was nearly fifteen, and practically grown-up. Joe would have to understand that Lisa wasn't his baby girl anymore.

Lisa went looking for Tracey. Tracey's Ma was brill. Let her wear lipstick and drink wine and all. When Tracey's Ma went to her aerobics, Wednesday nights they went round to Tracey's and watched mad films about sex. The films belonged to Tracey's Ma's last boyfriend who had hidden them in the attic and forgotten all about them.

Sometimes when Tracey had a fella in she'd want the place to herself so Lisa had to stay at home and watch **Coronation Street** instead.

Tracey thought Lisa was daft to worry about her Da after Paul asking her to the disco and all. And him dead gorgeous, the spit of Colin Farrell. Imagine Paul picking Lisa when he could have anyone he wanted.' *Tell your Da to fuck off* said Tracey. *'It's your life.'*

'She has her heart set on this disco.'
'And what did you say?'
'Said I'd ask you.'
He flapped his newspaper impatiently, like washerwoman folding sheets. *'She's not goin' - and that's final.'*

He turned up the television, drowning out her protests. The back of his neck was red with temper. On the screen, a bony, blonde transvestite told crude jokes in a hoarse, Lancashire accent. Joe laughed loudly, falsely, hunching his shoulders away from her. She stood up.

'I'm going to bed.'
'That's right, sulk.' He turned to look at her. *' It was your idea as much as mine to make her wait until she's sixteen.'*

'Times change, Joe. She's a sensible girl.' Her voice softened. *'I don't want her to be a laughing stock with her pals. And it's the last day of term. She promised not to ask again until the summer.'*

She ran a finger around the back of his neck, tracing his ear-lobe lightly with her thumb. *'She's gone round to Tracy for an hour-we have the house to ourselves.'*

When Lisa got home the kitchen was in darkness. Da must be in a right temper. Miserable bastard. She poured milk, sat cross-legged on the floor stroking the cat. She thought of Paul, coming up to her at break, in front of everybody, his mouth smiling. *'C'mon, Lisa. Tell the ould fella he has to let you out of the playpen sometime.'*

'Jaysus,' said Tracey,' *if it was me I'd climb out the winda, I'm not jokin'.'*

'Yeah,' said Lisa. *'Brill idea that. I suppose you'd ask me Da to hold the ladder.'*

'You can go to Dizzies.' Her mother, bleary-eyed, buttered toast with thick, practised swipes.

'You're not jokin' me Ma?'

'I'm not jokin'. I'll expect all 'A's' in the Christmas test, mind.'

'Ma, you can have the whole alphabet.'

New boots, mini-skirt, lip-gloss, underwear, the lot.

'Don't tell your father, that's two weeks housekeeping.'

Even Tracey thought she looked cool. *'New knickers and all.'* She smiled knowingly *'Hope Paul likes pink.'* Tossing them in the air, catching them in one careless hand. *'Ah, Jaysus, would you look at the wan blushin'?'*

She painted her nails three times. Couldn't find her lip-gloss. Her hair was a mess. Paul phoned at five. *'See you on the bus, babe.'*

Babe.

She sat at the foot of the stairs, smiling to herself, cradling the sound of his voice in her head.

Babe.

Nobody could be this happy. Could they?

'You can't wear that yoke.'

'Why not?'
'You can see your arse.'
'Don't look at it then.'
'Don't be so lippy, Miss, or you'll be staying in the house.'
'Go easy on her Joe-I wore shorter myself.'
' That's right-encourage her. When she gets into bother don't come whingin' to me.'

The lights of the mini-bus come scurrying round the corner, like small animals running from the dark. Ma insisting on leaving her to the bus-stop. Imagine. She stands apart, rigid with shame.
'Good-bye love.'
'Bye, Ma.'
Blinded by the lights, the soft, smoky fug, Paul's smile.
'Enjoy yourself, pet. Be careful.'
Paul's arm around her, the smoke from his cigarette stinging her eyes. *'I like the boots.'* His hand sliding up her thigh. Smothered giggles, everybody watching.
'Fancy a Pepsi, Lisa?' And someone passes the familiar can over her shoulder.
The drink slides down her throat, searing, catching her breath. The warmth coils itself neatly in the pit of her stomach, like a sleepy snake. Nice. It feels nice. She shares the fag with Paul, from his mouth to hers. Intimate. The word flutters around in her head like a trapped moth. His hand is warm on her thigh, laying claim. His tongue licking at the corners of her lips, gentle, insistent, greedy as a cat.
The can is passed again. Someone begins to sing. 'Tell me what you want, what you really, really want.' The voice breathy and mocking. His fingers drum gently on

her breast, she moves uneasily, hears Tracey's mocking *'Mammy's little sweetheart.'* She slumps down .nobody watching anyway all kissing and moaning and giggling and Paul's thumb circles her nipple, round and round and round.

Queues edging towards alighted doorway through the friendly half-dark. Inside the noise and the heat hit her like a slap. She clings to Paul, his tongue deep in her mouth, and holds frantically to the bulwark of his strength with her splayed hands.

'Wait here,' and she stands obediently in the half-dark, waiting. She shivers violently; bereft of his shelter. She wraps her arms around her bare shoulders and watches faces dip in and out of the shadows, a kaleidoscope of mouths and cheeks and closed eyes.

She feels his warmth behind her and he slides an arm around her waist and cradles her in the angle of his shoulder. Presses something into her hand. *'Here.'* Watching the sudden terrified bewilderment on her face.

'Jaysus, Lisa, lighten up. It's only something' to give you a buzz. Not E or anythin'- I'm not that fuckin' stupid.'

She reaches the cloakroom and sways as she leans against the grimy basin, sticky with sweat. The walls gather and recede round her. Oh, God, she's going to be sick. She gets her head in the bowl just in time. When she stands up her face is chalky white in the mirror. Must be the lights.

Paul watches her weaving towards the door -spider's webs of vomit trailing viscously from her chin. He shrugs-he's no fuckin' nurse. Beside him, a redhead hitches a grubby strap hopefully over one thin shoulder. Nice lookin' chick-might as well try his luck. Looks like Lisa is out of it for the night. Green as grass Lisa, don't know why he bothered in the first place. The redhead settles herself against him like a homing pigeon. He curves his hand under her buttocks and closes his eyes.

Lisa's head is on fire, hands freezing. She wants to lie down. Can't miss the bus-Da would have a fit.

'*Cover your arse.*' She leans on the wall; the rough stone biting into her arms, and watches the grass swell and billow around her, like waves on a restless sea.

Find the bus. Just a little rest first. '*See you on the bus babe.*' Blackness gathers against the corner of the wall, threatening to engulf her. It swells menacingly and she whimpers, sinking to her knees in the friendly shadows, hiding from the threatening dark.

The bus shudders into reluctant life.
'*Hey, Paul, where's Lisa?*'
'*How the fuck would I know.*'
'*What happened to the redhead?*'
Collected by a big bruiser in an Audi, that's what. He remembers how she pulled away from him, her eyes big with fear. '*I'll have to go-it's me Da.*' Pulling the thin nylon down quickly to cover childish, almost non-existent breasts.

He ignores the catcalls. The lights are dimmed. Presently he sleeps.

'*What time is it?*'
'*Gone half two.*'
'*I'll bloody kill her.*'
'*You're sure she wasn't on the bus? Asleep, maybe.*'
'*I got on the bloody bus. The boyfriend was there alright. Asleep with his mouth open. Mumblin' something about an Audi.*'

Her hands shake, she clasps them together for comfort-the nails digging into her palms. *'Go and look for her Joe, she might have missed the bus altogether.'*

'I'll warm her arse for her when I get my hands on her. That's the last time she's leavin' this house until she's finished school.'

He shrugs into his jacket, his eyes flat with terror. The door slams behind him and she can feel the house shiver in the returning silence.

She pours tea, watches oily pictures gather on its cooling surface. Her skin feels raw, as if she had been flayed. In the attic, pipes grumble. She listens to the pitiless roar of traffic sweeping past her gate. A cat cries out in a neighbour's garden. The clock ticks......

FOR BETTER OR WORSE

The morning began exactly the same as any other, with the quiet dawn exploding into a cacophony of alarm clocks, Britney Spears and Westlife slugging it on the twin's radios, angry banging on the bathroom door.

Paddy, drinking his usual hurried cup of coffee, didn't even notice. He stood in the middle of the untidy kitchen, elegant and remote in a perfectly tailored suit. Ignoring the jumble of discarded pyjamas and wails about unlaundered sports kit and lost homework, side-stepping sleepy children as he grabbed his briefcase and left, already speaking urgently into his mobile phone as the front door thudded behind him.

His big, expensive car purred down the driveway and disappeared into the distance. I'd once sold a garnet ring, inherited from my grandmother; to pay for our first car, a twenty-year-old Ford with holes in the floor. Now Paddy drove in lavish, leather -upholstered luxury and I wore a diamond solitaire on my hand. A gift to celebrate his first big contract.

'Thanks,' he had said, sliding the ring over my wedding band, hiding and overwhelming the cheap gold with its opulent beauty. *'Thanks for everything.'*

Sixteen-year-old Lizzie, in the throes of first love, sat with hunched shoulders, scowling at the cat as if he had mortally offended her. I ignored the uniform skirt hitched unevenly above her knees, the uneven streaks of lurid pink in her beautiful, blonde, hair. Lizzie blamed her headmistress's 'no make–up in school' policy, for the fact that object of her devotion, a spotted, gangly youth she called 'Jonner' had so, far, failed to notice her existence. Miss Dillon, an attractive, dynamic fifty year old, was, according to Lizzie, being totally unreasonable in refusing to allow her to wear her school blouse unbuttoned to the navel, a stud in her nose, high heeled, leather boots.

'*What would she know about love?*' Lizzie demanded sulkily just last night. '*She's just jealous because she's so old.*'

She grabbed a piece of cold toast and rushed off with a half-hearted wave, slamming the front door shut behind her.

I dispensed lunches, bus fares, kisses, reciting the daily mantra of love and worry.

'*Bye now, take care, look after your sister.*' The ten year old twins blew self-conscious kisses and ran down the path with Jodie, who was only six, trotting doggedly behind them, like a small, determined shadow.

I tidied the bathroom, grateful for the dubious tranquillity of familiar boredom. In Lizzie's room the dainty, flower sprigged wallpaper was barely visible under the jumble of posters of football heroes and sullen looking, leather-clad pop stars. I smoothed sheets and folded discarded clothing and closed the door again on a room that was full of Lizzie's secrets.

Laura's bunk bed was piled high with bedraggled-looking furry toys. Gillian's was smooth and spotless, the books on the shelf beside her bed arranged in neat, regimented rows. Yet in looks the twins were practically identical, tall and blonde and blue-eyed, like Lizzie. Of all our children only Jodie resembled his father - dark haired and handsome, with wicked, hazel eyes.

I made coffee and stood by the kitchen window in a pool of sunlight and watched a blackbird on the lawn rocking back on yellow heels as he tugged at a reluctant worm. I turned on the radio and closed my eyes for a moment as the cool notes of a Bach melody fell like drops of water into the silence.

The day stretched pleasurably before me. Gardening, shopping, a chance to read a favourite magazine. I hoped Paddy would be able to make it home for dinner. Just lately he seemed to be working extra-long hours.

'*The price of success,*' he'd said ruefully, when I'd complained. '*We're in the middle of a boom; I have to make the most of it.*'

Ten minutes later I listened to the sound of his car coming up the driveway, then the crunch of gravel and the muffled slam of the driver's door.

He stood in the doorway, his briefcase clasped before him like a shield, watching me with thoughtful, pitying eyes. His nails were manicured, buffed to a dull expensive shine. When had Paddy begun to look after his hands? I swept crumbs surreptitiously into my cupped palm, a part of my mind ridiculing my uneasy awareness of my unlipsticked mouth, bare feet, the comfortable shabbiness of old clothes. This was my husband, for heaven's sake. Paddy -my boy from the building site who, for years had shared shepherd's pie and cheap wine and the dread of unpaid bills. Had held my hand through three, sweaty, sticky labours and kept watch with me through a heart-stopping vigil over a desperately sick child.

Watching me now with the hostile eyes of a stranger.

'*Did you forget something?*'

'*I've met someone else, I'm leaving you.*'

The last notes of the music fell with a sudden uneasy flurry into the stillness.

'Her name is Janice.'

The silence sagged between us.

'We both tried to fight it Kate, but it was no use. We just couldn't.'

Suddenly, incongruously, I wanted to laugh at the sheer banality of his words.

'This thing is bigger than both of us.' I registered the shocked outrage on his face and realised that I'd spoken aloud. He frowned.

'Please, Kate, this is serious.'

'I know,' I said, *'I know.'*

I could hear the calm detachment to my own voice - like an actress reading someone else's script. I sat with my hands folded in my lap, listening attentively, nodding like a clockwork doll while my gentle knight carefully laid before me the armour that was to cushion the wounds of war.

He was offering me a generous allowance, the house, the second car, the Premium Bonds that were held in my name, because I was the lucky one, the winner of charity draws and Christmas raffles.

He and Janice were moving into a penthouse apartment in the better part of town.

The children's school fees would be his responsibility of course.

Of course.

I followed him upstairs and watched as he packed, tumbling clothes haphazardly on the bed, murmuring urgently into the mobile phone clamped between ear and hunched shoulder. I picked up an unfamiliar tie. Grey silk, slashed with crimson. I rolled it up and balanced it in the palm of my hand where it lay, coiled like a sleeping snake.

He stowed his suitcase in the back seat of the car and then stood in the doorway, watching me with defiantly tilted chin, like a small boy who had been caught stealing biscuits. The toes of his hand-made shoes gleamed like freshly fallen conkers

'I'll collect the rest later.'

I told the children that evening. *'Don't worry,'* I said, *'everything is going to be fine, I promise.'* Silently raging at the death of innocence in their bewildered eyes.

I told neither family nor friends, refusing to justify the horror of his betrayal with the substance of a name. At night, I walked while the children slept, hugging my grief to me as I trudged through the friendly dark. The house welcomed me home, stirring and sighing in sympathy, as I lay sleepless, holding me safe in the shelter of its familiar walls.

Paddy phoned regularly, enquiring courteously about my wellbeing, asking if he could speak to the children.

'I'll just call them.' I said, *'They're doing homework - everything's fine.'*

I learned to dance to a different rhythm. Closed my mind to empty spaces and the sharpness of unexpected grief. The poignancy of finding a carefully hoarded Valentine, an odd sock, Christmas cards addressed to Kate and Paddy, Paddy and Kate.

A letter came from the bank addressed to Ms Kate Cleary. My name, under the bank's logo, looked unbearably sad. I threw it in the fire, unopened.

I found a solicitor; a brisk young woman who assured me cheerfully that we would take him for everything we could get. A sign hung over her desk. **'SUE THE**

BASTARD ', it said, in curly Gothic writing in a heavy silver frame.

The machinery of the divorce courts creaked on with agonizing slowness. Paddy picked up the children at regular intervals, raising his hand to me in greeting and farewell. They returned, shame-faced and defiant, wearing expensive trainers, flaunting jeans with designer logos. They never mentioned Janice's name.

I took a job in an accountant's office and hired a childminder, a motherly, middle-aged woman called Rose. I sometimes joined colleagues for lunch or, when Rose could be persuaded to stay a little later, an occasional drink. I began to go out with a man I'd met through work. Robert was a widower; kind and attentive and good-looking. I even enjoyed getting dressed up again, having my hair done in a different style, seeing the admiration in a man's eyes. Jodie and the twins tolerated Robert with cheerful indifference. Lizzie loathed him. After a few weeks we parted amicably, with no real regret.

It was summer again when Paddy phoned and invited me to lunch. We had to talk, he said insistently, there were still so many unresolved issues between us. Unresolved issues -the jargon of therapists and lawyers, the well-heeled sharp suited professionals who had, between them, dismantled my world.

He named the restaurant where we would meet, a place that was too expensive, too exclusive, to have held any of our shared memories.

I put down the phone and sat with the dogs' smooth, golden head against my knee, listening to the muffled sounds of the world outside my door.

He stood when he saw me, smiling and holding my chair for me with practised charm. Apart from occasional glimpses I hadn't seen him in over a year. He looked tired, the lines from mouth to chin more firmly etched. I noticed the shorn elegance of his once curly hair, the subdued gleam of the silk tie that was the silvery grey of a gull's wing. I was glad I had dressed up, had dismissed my first childish impulse to arrive, tousled and un-made-up, in a tracksuit.

'*You look well.*' I said and he smiled, patting the flatness of his stomach with a wry grimace.

'*It's an effort –I'm a permanent fixture in the gym these days.*'

He drank mineral water and waved away the sweet trolley with a shame-faced grin. Paddy, who once boasted he could eat apple tarts for Ireland?

I drank three glasses of wine and ate with surprising hunger.

'*You look wonderful,*' he said. '*The children tell me you're doing fine.*'

'*You shouldn't be discussing me with the children.*'

'*I miss you.*'

'*I'll bet.*'

'*You've changed.*' It sounded almost like an accusation. He leaned forward suddenly and caught my hands between his own, his muscled, labourer's body moving uneasily on the delicate chair. A vein throbbed in the dark, shadowed hollow of his throat.

'*Kate.*' he said urgently '*Please, Kate. Janice and me–it's all over.*'

I looked down at our clasped hands, saw the polished gleam of his fingernails against the raw strength of callused fingers and thought of the days I'd endured without him, the long nights I'd lain awake listening to the sound of children sobbing in the dark. This sophisticated stranger who had once been my husband.

'You've changed,' he said again. I watched the sadness grow in his eyes and my heart sighed with pity and finally broke.

THE SOUND OF MANY WATERS

'*Don't be such an oddity,*' said Breedeen, '*what harm would it do you if you were to come to the dance. Couldn't you just sit and listen to the music?*'

She was twisting the seams of her nylons, trying to hide the ladder that ran up the back of her stout little leg, the white flesh of her back and shoulders spilling over her bodice. She turned her head, laughing at me across her shoulder.

Oh, I could, Breedeen, indeed I could. I could sit and listen to the music and the whole parish could stand back and admire my fine shapely legs and the black curls tumbling down my back and my green eyes and my gouged, unfinished mouth, twisted and puckered so that people crossed themselves and called on God to bless the mark of my misfortune and the children ran after me chanting. '*Kitty the hare, Kitty the hare,*' in their sweet, spiteful voices.

'*Someone has to stay at home and keep an eye on the old fella.*'

Breedeen pursed her mouth and blew phantom kisses at her face in the mirror

'*You might be sorry. Andy Shanaghy will be looking for you when they play the lady's choice.*'

'*You'll be well fit to manage Andy without me.*'

I watched her dab crimson lip salve onto her mouth with her finger She wiped the stained finger carelessly on her stocking top and tucked stray wisps of reddish hair impatiently into her armpits.

'*Will I do?*'

'*You'll have every man in the place wild for you.*'

'*There's not a decent man among the lot of them. You won't be missing much.*'

'*Except Conar?*'

'*Except Conar.*'

Smug dimples came and went on Breeden's cheeks and she wrapped her arms around herself and hugged her dumpy, little body that was as warm, as comfortable, as an armful of sleepy cats. Her fat buttocks in their washed-out rayon knickers pressed slyly together, like children sharing a secret.

She looked at me sideways.

'*I hate going into the hall on my own. Everyone turning to look at you. I only hope to God Conar doesn't let me down. I'm not coming up that lane on my own. I'd rather stay at the road gate for the night than face up that lane in the dark.*'

She took her good dress from the back of the chair and pulled it over her head and twirled around the room in a kaleidoscope of cheap cotton and the acrid smell of sweat and half-washed feet rose from around her like a mist.

'*Keep a good eye on the ould fella.*' And then she was gone, laughing, stuffing a flash lamp into her coat pocket as she went.

I leaned out the opened window and watched the moon sidestepping over the ditches and silvering the river field. The tops of the pines behind the hayshed were sharp and savage looking against the sky.

I could hear the rattle of her bike going down the lane and the high-pitched defiance in her voice as she sang her way round by the Hangman's Gap, her lamp playing hide and seek through the whin bushes on Kiernan's hill.

Then the sound of her singing died and there was nothing but the forlorn lowing of a cow and the sound of the Erne winding its way along beside the river field, whispering itself to sleep.

I went into the kitchen and turned down the lamp and poked the fire, swinging the heavy black kettle over the wakening flames. In the corner my father was sleeping, slack-mouthed in his chair. His lips were a wet, mottled purple, like the entrails of a dead animal. I made tea and woke him. He took the tea without speaking and swallowed it in a long, toothless slobber. Then he levered himself up painfully and unhooked his brown rosary from the nail beside the chimneybreast.

'I'm going to my bed. Let you leave the door on the latch for Breedeen.'

'I will,' I said. *'Goodnight Dada.'*

He didn't answer me. The room door closed behind him with a sad sulky sigh.

I rinsed the mug, thinking of Breeden getting off her bicycle outside the hall and going in the door to lights and warmth and music. The whole parish would be there, the drunk and the sober and the desperate- old maids in prim cotton dresses with lined, hopeful faces and bachelors slouched up against the wall, their shy, sin-shackled loins loosened by the drink and the sight of the women's bare arms sheened with sweat in the light from dusty, fly-speckled bulbs. Hoping against hope for the chance to grope a girl in a neighbour's hayshed when the music was over and the dancers all gone home. Not a decent man among them, Breedeen said.

Except Conar.

I stared into the fire and I could her Breedeen's voice in my head, 'Andy Shanaghy will be watching out for you,' her words rippled with laughter. Andy, the parish bastard, his red neck that was covered in boils rising out of a stiff, white collar, clicking his way round the floor with some desperate old maid, as rigid as a clockwork soldier. Andy Shanaghy taking pity on poor hare-lipped Cissie while Conar whirled past with Breedeen in his arms and his black head etched against the dirty yellow walls, like the head of a king on some old coin.

I thought once that my black hair and my straight back and the bit of land that was coming to me would be enough to balance out the misfortune of my face. Times when I'd meet Conar on the road and he'd lie on the ditch at the side of the meadow gate, telling me about the lonesomeness of life for a labourer in the great cities of England. His eyes razing my father's narrow fields while the two of us leaned back shoulder to shoulder, listening to the river gossiping away to itself beside us.

'You're a queer girl, Cissie. Sitting here on your lonesome listening to the river.'

'It talks a lot more sense than some of the things I have to listen to above up in the house from Breedeen and my father.'

Conar laughed. *'The sound of many waters.'* he said. *'That's what ould Harrison, the Presbyterian, does be saying to my mother when she sings below in the bog and her spreading turf.'*

He closed his eyes and his voice deepened.

'And her voice is like the sound of many waters.' He opened his eyes and looked at me, laughing. *'She sings 'Kevin Barry' to vex him.'*

We laughed together at poor, contrary Harrison and I wished and wished that I could go down and hear his mother singing on the bog and that I could go up to the hall for the dance and be tumbled in the shadowed ditches in Conar's arms.

My mother died when I was nine, worn out by my father's temper and his endless drunken rantings about the mark of God on poor Cissie's face. When his fourth child, a boy, was stillborn my grandmother swore that he cursed my mother into her grave for failing to give him a son. When she died I was the one who was left to carry the burden of his bitterness, kept away from school at the age of twelve to cook and clean and help on the farm and rear two small sisters with the grudging help of neighbours. I learned early to lock my door against his lonesome, bellowed warnings as he came swaying up the lane from Biddy Mac's, beating his fists against the gable wall in self-pitying rage. Glaring down at the false, moon washed glamour of his few shabby acres and crying that he had no son, no son, and God had cursed him surely for turning his back on his own class and marrying a Maguire.

Saintly Joanie, the youngest, ran away to the shelter of the Presentation nuns when she was seventeen, her red face alight with sanctity and the price of the roany cow tucked safely in the waistband of her drawers. Serene in the certainty of her calling and her reward in the world to come.

It was very late when Breedeen came home. She sat on the edge of the bed, her eyes shining in the half-darkness, hung around with a curious smell of sweat and excitement as she shook me into wakefulness.

'Conar is coming up tomorrow to ask the ould fella.'

Cutting the quiet night to ribbons with the sharpness of her whispers.

'Ask him what?'

'If he can marry me.'

I closed my eyes. The sound of his voice as he told me that his mother sang 'Kevin Barry' on the bog, his dark eyes and wild black hair, the tender blue veins stark against the whiteness of the inside of his elbow, like roads mapped through the terrain of some nameless country.

'You're gone very quiet-can't you say something?'

'It's a bit sudden. What hurry is on you?'

Breedeen laughed, a high nervous titter.

'I'm over two months gone, I'm beginning to show already.' She laughed again.

'The ould fella will go mad but it can't be helped. I'll be the full of my bib by Christmas.'

The night before they got married she asked me for my mother's wedding ring.

'It's not as if you'll ever have much use for it.' Her face was blank with unconscious cruelty.

She was married in a pink suit that was tight cross her breasts and when Conar put my mother's ring on her hand his bowed, black head was dappled with the light that showered from the tall, stained glass windows behind the high altar.

We drove them to the station in the pony and trap, Breedeen's pudgy fingers curled possessively in the crook of her new husband's elbow. They were going to Bundoran for a week. She hung out the window, waving, until the train was out of sight.

'Let you go into the hotel and wait for me,' my father ordered. *'I have a bit of business to finish up in the town.'*

That evening when we were finished the milking he handed me a thick brown envelope, his eyes full of belligerent shame.

'There's four hundred pounds in that envelope. Let you put it away against a time of want or misfortune, for by God, it was hard earned, every copper penny.'

He grunted, avoiding my eyes. 'When the young pair come back from their gallivanting, I'll have to go back again to the town with the whole lot of you and sort out this business of the land. But you'll have your own place in this house – you need have no fear of that. A roof over your head and your bed and board and whatever few pound that's left in the bank when I'm gone.'

The day after they came home we went back to the town as he had promised and he signed over the farm to Conar, the pen gouging in the thick paper and a clock ticking dustily away in a darkened corner.

They moved into the lower room and I slept in the loft on a truckle bed. Sometimes I'd lie awake until dawn, listening to the sound of fumblings and creakings and smothered laughter from the room beneath. Breedeen wanted no more to do with the land. She took over the kitchen and made bread and hung Conar's socks to dry on the crook of the fire with small, proprietary pats. Bustling around him as we came in from the milking or asking me to help her straighten the blankets on the big, feather bed, her belly rounding and her mouth curling with remembered pleasure.

In May their dark haired son was born. All that Summer she lay in bed late while I turned hay alongside Conar in the river field or spent long sun-filled days on the bog with my bare legs tickled by drifts of meadowsweet, listening to the sly whispering breezes in the heather, watched the sweat beading on his back and the smooth ripple of the muscles of his thighs and feeling the gut clenching ache in my belly as I prayed silently.

'*Immaculate Heart of Mary, keep me pure in thought and deed.*' The words that were written on my mother's memory card in silver ink. Imploring Heavenly forgiveness for every damp rush of desire, watching the long curves of his back bent in graceful indifference over the rows of turf that lay like dead soldiers in the sun.

My father had kept his promise. I had my bed against the wall in the lower room where I lay and listened to the milky snufflings of children sleeping soundly in a tumble of frowsy blankets. A warm coat and good strong shoes and the full of her belly for poor, hare-lipped Cissie that was so good to Breedeen and Joanie and Dada when Mammy died.

And down the years we went. Children being born and my father dying ignominiously in the fort field curled in a heap of vomit and cow's shit while the children played unheedingly on the grass beside him.

We buried him beside my mother. I stood by the grave and watched Breedeen as she wept noisily against Conar's shoulder with their four sons gathered around her, the youngest clinging to her hand that was mottled purple with the cold. Childbearing had aged her, had turned the pretty, plump bride into a fat middle-aged woman, grown old before her time.

My father left her three hundred pounds in his will. She nagged Conar to buy a car before the children got their deaths going to Mass in the bad weather and eventually he bought an old Ford Anglia from a neighbour and they began to attend the twelve o'clock Mass in his own neighbouring parish of Cormona. They ate their Sunday dinner in his mother's house, and afterwards he went down to the pub to play cards and watch the hurling on a grainy black and white television.

It was late ,near the children's bedtime, by the time they finally got home.

Joanie wrote a long time afterwards from her convent in Africa, signing her letter 'Your sister in Jesus Christ, Mother Mary Jerome.' Breedeen shook the flimsy envelope and two pictures fell out, one of Saint Teresa, the Little Flower, with her arms full of pink roses and the other a poem by Brian O'Higgins with blue and yellow flowers curling around the border.

'Not one red shilling,' she said. *'The nuns know how to hold on to their money. And I'm left to bury her poor father. Him that was so good to Joanie. Didn't he give her price of the roany heifer, the best milker in the byre, and she running off to her convent and leaving the hardship behind her?'*

Pakie, the baby, swung out of his mother's apron and whined that he wanted the lovely pictures, could he have them ah, could he Mammy until she lost patience and caught the child a stinging blow on his fat cheek and said he could wipe his arse with them for all she cared.

Now that my Sundays were my own , I hoarded them jealously against the days spent in the crowded foetid kitchen surrounded by the children's snot nosed whinings, the dark murmur of Conar's voice as he muttered excuses and went away to the town, Breedeen's peevish complaints, the cry of a slapped child as she waddled around the little room wiping tears from a small face with the corner of her apron, berating Conar with low-voiced venom, spitting the words from the corner of her mouth as if she was glad to be rid of their bitterness.

I woke early, walking the three miles to first Mass with half the parish still only stretching in its sleep. Down the stony lane that clung to like an anxious child to its mother's skirts with my breath misting before me like some friendly ghost. The church was always half empty. A few anxious mothers, shopkeepers and publicans, trying to fit God into the crowded hours of their busy lives. The church was quiet on these early mornings, nothing but the insistent tap-tap of the branches against the high stained glass windows and the slow guttering of candles. I sat alone under the shadow of the pulpit, gathering the quiet spaciousness around me like a cloak. And home again and opening the kitchen door on the blessed silence.

I'd go to the loft and open my mother's open American trunk which held the white bedspread and linen cloths for laying out the dead. Feeling for the brown envelope that still held the money my father had given me. I'd take out my velvet dress that I'd bought long ago with the price of a lamb I sold to a neighbour. I told my father the animal had been drowned in the river. I'd brought the dress home from the town and hidden it away up under the rafters long before Conar came up the lane to ask if he could marry Breedeen and work the land and be my father's son.

I crept downstairs again with the dress whispering and sliding against my skin. And down in the fort field I'd dance where the river twisted away towards the town, listening to its music, held safe in the crook of its shining elbow. Close my eyes and wrap my two arms around my body, swaying and feeling the imagined strength of him under my splayed hands until some sound warned me-the hum of a car on the lower road, a flurry of leaves, the drum roll of a flight of pheasants startled from their nest. I'd slip back up the hill, shivering like a sleepwalker, my body cold from the imagined loss of his shelter.

Until the day the door swung open in the middle of a summer storm as I swayed and sang through the shadowed kitchen in my green dress.

I felt the slap of cold air against my legs and I opened my eyes to the sight of Breedeen, slack mouthed, her belly trembling with laughter. *'Sweet mother of the divine God, have you lost your reason entirely?'*

She chugged into the kitchen, her fat, red face beaded with rain and sweat. Conar followed her, carrying a wan, listless child against his shoulder.

She draped her wet scarf over the airing rack and pushed a chair against the wall with her knee. *'Bring that child over here beside the fire like good man, 'til I put a sup of something warm in his stomach.'* She glanced at me, her eyes bright with malice. *'The poor wee lad got sick in his Granny's-though it wasn't all he got to eat, God help him.'*

She fussed over the child, shot a sly look at Conar. *'Are you taking a good look at the get up of poor Cissie, dressed up like a lady and dancing around the kitchen with the invisible man?'*

I climbed the stairs to the loft, ignoring her shouted instructions to get blankets, bring the rest of the children out of the car, make a drop of tea for herself and Conar. I sat on the edge of the trunk and buried my outspread fingers against the mossy folds of my skirt. I could hear her soft grumbling to the sick child, the bewildered yelp of the dog being pushed out into the rain. Conar said something to the child. His voice was slow and gentle.

I went downstairs still wearing the dress and watched her buttering bread, her mouth pursed with suppressed laughter. She poured tea for Conar, passing no more heed on me than if I were the cat. The child slept, pale faced and peaceful, in my father's chair. I poured my own tea, taking my mug from its hook at the top of the dresser and she looked at me, her eyes glossy with hate. *'Cavorting around the kitchen in a dress that must have cost twenty pounds and here's me with not a stitch to wear to my own cousin's wedding.'* She slammed down her mug. *'You're the sly damsel and no mistake, taking the bread out of the mouths of them that gave you shelter.'* She slapped the kettle on the range and small gobbits of water hissed angrily on its hot surface. The fat folds of her neck looked like pursed mouths.

'What use would the like of you have for a velvet dress? Did you think some eejit would be so busy admiring it that he might miss your mouth altogether?' The child stirred and whimpered. She bent over him, shushing him softly.

'I took nothing of yours,' I said, *'I spent my own money.'* I watched the greed grow in her eyes. *'That dress would be no good to you anyway,'* I said, *'It wouldn't go up on your leg, never mind your waist.'*

Conar stood up and gathered the milking buckets from beside the dresser. *'I'll leave you to fight it out among yourselves so. The cows have to be milked, no matter what comes or goes.'*

He paused in the doorway, his eyes flickering over her fat, shapeless body. *'Put a green dress on that arse and be thinking I was after getting another field, with the width of you.'*

The door closed on an angry little *'phut'*. The child woke and climbed from the chair and buried his face in Breedeen's dress. She held him against her hip with a fat, reddened hand. *'Go out and help that poor man with the milking, it's little enough you do to earn your keep.'*

The byre was musty with the smell of animal bodies and hay. He was hunkered under the black heifer, his head resting easily against her silky flank. I listened to the milk plinking into the bucket like the tentative, one-fingered tinkle of a piano. He didn't turn his head. *'You take Bessie, this little lassie is uneasy still.'* He quieted the animal with soft murmurs. We worked silently while the milk rose and made lacy caps around the bucket's edges.

I left him to finish the milking by himself and walked down to the river field in the rain. Breedeen had the land and Conar's sons and lay with him in my mother's bed, wearing my mother's ring. I resolved to write to Joanie. I'd offer the nuns my father's money and a strong pair of hands in return for shelter and food. It would be no worse of a bargain than living out the rest of my days on the periphery of other people's lives. I saw a life of charity and duty stretching away before me like a grey ribbon. The children growing up and going away and leaving the three of us to fester together into bitter old age. Or worse, Breedeen dying before me and leaving me to care for another drink-sodden ruin.

I remembered her wedding day, the smug roundness of her belly, my mother's ring shining on her hand. The first few months of being near him while his dark eyes followed Breedeen around the kitchen, watching her anxious glances at the slow, tortured ticking of the clock until I escaped at last from the smothered passion on their faces and come running here instead, to the river field to sit in the soft darkness and listen to the river lulling the fields to sleep.

When I went back she was sitting beside the fire, her hands folded in her lap. Her face was swollen and mottled as if she had been crying. *'You look perished,'* she said, almost kindly, *'Sit down and I'll make a sup of tea to warm the two of us.'*

'*I didn't hear the car,*' I said, '*is Conar gone away to the town?*'

She lifted her head sharply, like an animal scenting danger but when she answered me her voice was calm. '*Conar has taken to his bed, God between us and all harm. The first Sunday night he missed out of Biddy Mac's in fifteen years. Will they be able to carry on without him, at all at all?*'

She smiled mistily and for a minute I remembered the girl she had been long ago, getting ready for the dance, before child bearing and indifference had pummelled her body into such sad, misshapen hopelessness.

We drank our tea in silence and then she put her mug down and took the hem of my dress gently between her fingers. '*You'd be as well to rinse that good dress before the dirt dries on it.*' She fondled the skirt between her finger and thumb, her face collapsing into wistfulness. '*It must be a grand thing all the same to have the feel of a dress like that against a body's skin.*'

I was at the room door when she spoke again.

'*I'm sorry if I was a bit hard on you. It must be a terrible thing to go through the world with your shape and make on you and the mark of an animal on your poor face. It's small wonder that you made up a sweetheart in your own head to go dancing round the kitchen floor and you with neither child nor man to call your own.*'

I washed the dress and folded it away under the white bedspread for laying out the dead. There would be no more dancing.

On Friday Breedeen went into the town. When she came home again she sat at the end of the kitchen table, tight-lipped and defiant, rapping the worn oilcloth with my mother's ring.

'*I brought that ould green dress into Tessie Curran's to see if she could let it out a bit for me under the arms, T'will save me having to buy a new dress for the wedding.*' The dull colour washed up her neck and face. '*Don't be looking at me like that Cissie-isn't as if you would have much use for it yourself. You're a bit long in the tooth now for dancing and playacting. God knows I have little enough left over to buy style for myself with an extra mouth to feed and four children growing like weeds out of every stitch of clothes on their backs.*'

Conar was in the byre, leaning against the low walls between the cattle stalls. I leaned up against the wall, watching the way the heavy lashes curled on his cheeks, like a child's.

'*She got her hands on the green dress.*'

His voice shivered with laughter. '*Tessie will have a job trying to get that to go around the size of that arse. The poor woman will be up all night.*'

'*It makes no differ,*' I said bitterly,' *where would I be going in a velvet dress?*'

'*You could dance below in the river field. You have a grand shape on you, dancing in that dress.*' He reached his arms out and held them rigidly on either side of me, trapping me against the wall. '*Twas only myself that saw you by chance a few times.*' He touched my puckered mouth with his thumb, smiling. '*Ah, Cissie, ah, Cissie, it's only a small thing.*'

'*It's no small thing to me,*' I said, '*It cost me a whole lifetime.*'

He flung the cigarette away and I watched it disintegrate with a hopeless, little hiss in a puddle of dirty water. '*You and me, both,*' he said, '*it cost both of us dear.*'

'*I'm leaving.*' I said. '*I made up my mind to write to Joanie and go away to the convent. I'm trained for nothing else. You should have had the place to yourselves this long time-I should have gone when my father died.'*

His fingers were bled white against my shoulder. I could hear the anger whorling through his voice. *'You'll go to no nuns. How long do you think a woman like yourself would last with that shower of dry-arsed bitches? There's nothing of the nun in you, Cissie. You'd light candles on the high altar with the sparks out of your two lovely eyes.'* His voice was sad. *'Breedeen gave you a hard time of it, letting you do the work of a man while she sat in the ashes with her diddies on her knees, smoking Woodbines.'*

I sank down on a milking school. I felt sick and light-headed with anger.

'You didn't do much to stop her.'

He hunkered down beside me. *'Didn't I have you beside me? You and the young ones. She wanted a man, the man that was yours.'*

'You were never my man, you wouldn't look the side of the road I was on.'

He was suddenly angry. *'You'd go nowhere to give a man a chance to look at you. Only to early Mass with your face hidden under a shawl, like a tinker woman begging for coppers. You'd go to no dance, did you expect me to do my courting below on the river bank, and you half-listening to the river.'*

'You're my sister's husband. She was expecting your child. It take two to make a child.'

'It takes too much porter and one unlucky night. I walked into her trap like a fly into a jam jar. I made a mistake, and by God I paid for it.'

He picked up a bucket and swung it against the uncomplaining flank of a cow. Refusing to look at me. His voice was pleading now.

'You and me Cissie, you and me? Down in the river field, just the two of us. I'll buy you a new dress, Cissie, the loveliest dress in the country. We'll dance, the pair of us, below in the river field and not one in the wide world will know of it only our two selves.'

His eyes were laughing. 'You said yourself that the Erne could make powerful music, if a body could be bothered to listen to it.'

I stood up and pushed roughly past him.

'You can finish up here without me. I'll write to Joanie in the morning.'

Breedeen was sitting by the kitchen fire, reading. She watched me warily from under her brows. 'You're not still vexed about that ould dress Cissie.'

'I am,' I said, 'I have every right to be vexed. You had no right to touch it, God knows I have little enough to call my own.'

She bridled, her eyes snapping. 'It's a bit late to be getting up on your high horse now and you owing me the bit that goes into your mouth and the roof over your head'.

She stood with her back to me and began to unhook mugs from the dresser. 'Let that be an end to it now. Tessie said the dress would be ready to be collected Friday.'

I went up to the loft, my throat tight with fear. I opened the trunk and saw the white bedspread rolled up roughly and pushed into a corner. There was a fifty pound note folded on top of it but the rest of the money and the envelope were gone.

Conar was in the kitchen, the car keys swinging from his fingers. I smiled into his eyes and turned to Breedeen. 'I have a few things to get in the town.'

His eyes danced back at me.

'What took you so long, woman-I was nearly away without you?'

When we walked out the door together she was bending over the fire, lighting a Woodbine from a spill of rolled up newspaper. She never even lifted her head.

THE BUTTERFLY JUG

It was quiet in the churchyard, with the peculiar hush of yew trees and old stone. In the street behind, buses trundled past tiredly in the heat. All around me well-muscled Germans walked with stolid earnestness among the dead, squinting obediently at the drunken headstones and grey forbidding walls.

A girl swung past, humming. She smiled in fleeting sympathy at the sight of my swollen stomach and tired face. The thin slats of the bench-pressed against my legs, cradling my bulk uneasily in its narrow lap. I watched her tight young body move with dancing ease through the sunshine, envying her grace.

The cathedral clock struck -greasy globules of sound in the heat. Four o'clock. I stirred unwillingly and the child kicked peevishly, catching me under the ribs. Time to go home to our small semi-detached jail with plastic Georgian mouldings flanking the narrow front door. Dusty flowerbeds where pansies choked quietly to death on the fumes of passing cars. Airless rooms. Nylon carpets and chipboard and the sound of a chair scraping on a neighbour's kitchen floor arrowing through the flimsy walls.

The child kicked again, vicious, demanding. I watched through a blur of self-pitying tears as pigeons fussed skittishly in the dust, like maiden aunts at a wedding. A blackbird seesawed precariously on a branch and crapped disdainfully at my feet. The pigeons fanned their wings and swept the flagstones with housewifely concern, their yellow eyes fixing the blackbird with unblinking disdain.

I walked uneasily down the shabby, sun-washed streets to the quays. The 51 bus gasped and shuddered to itself as it waited. Inside, the heat wrapped itself around me like a rubber blanket. People shifted uneasily on the sticky plastic of the seats, stared at the river, avoiding each other's eyes.

A lithe young man appeared, whistling, and swung himself into the high cab with the easy agility of a monkey. I stared out of the window, watching the river slip past. The bus swayed with the easy arrogance of a sailor, swinging its way around the corners, bullying a careless path through the thickening traffic. It tore down the hill into Inchicore and trembled to a halt. I lurched forward, the damp plastic seating peeling from between my shoulders like a second skin. The driver ducked from his seat, shrugging narrow, uncompromising shoulders. Broken down, he said. Wait for the next one. Or walk. The flat, unrelenting vowels of Cavan in his voice. He strolled to the front of the bus, lighting a cigarette as he went. He leaned against the shining grille, the blue smoke from his cigarette signalling his indifference to the thin air.

A fat woman, her face red with heat and anger, gathered her shopping bags and wheezed painfully to her feet and limped away, swollen ankles spilling from too-small shoes, mouthing helpless obscenities as she walked.

The pavement was littered with dusty crisp packets, lottery tickets shredded in a disillusioned fury, a Harp can crushed to blue and gold oblivion. A child teethered past on roller-skates, almost knocking me over. A taxi cruised slowly by, mocking me with its cool emptiness.

Behind me the deep dimness of a shop doorway beckoned and cajoled.

A bell tinkled in the half-darkness with a sound like water over pebbles. Glass and old china gleamed from the shelves. Pictures jostled and huddled against each other, propped against walls and odd pieces of furniture. Prim faced Victorians and polished apples and the iridescent blue-green glint of the throat feathers of a dead pheasant. A silver carriage clock pinged importantly on a high shelf. The sound punched small, shining holes in the quiet.

The jug sat on a small table by the window, its fat out-thrust lip laughing at me, the rounded belly seeming to shake with silent mirth. Butterflies, brown and cinnamon like the heart of a clover, dipped and hovered through painted daisies, their frail wings eternally suspended on the brink of flight.

I walked home with the jug cradled in my arms-haggled down to seventeen pounds-the last of the housekeeping money. Stifling guilt and trepidation as I passed the tall factories and freshly desecrated flower-fields. Strong shouldered young men moved easily through the greyness of brick and mortar. Bred to the hills of Kerry and the bogs of Mayo, whistling their indifference to the dead fields around them. Good money and the craic were mighty and double time for Saturdays.

I turned into the familiar street. Regimented rows of tasselled blinds. Stunted lilacs and sagging wrought-iron gates. No car in the driveway. Dan was working late again. Reprieve.

Emptiness came tumbling down the narrow stirs to meet me. In the kitchen the kettle stared blindly through

141

the uncurtained window, a note from Dan propped against the spout.

I unwrapped the jug tenderly, my fingers savouring its laughing curves. I stood it carefully on the window ledge and watched as the rays of late evening sun tickled the painted butterflies to glowing, exuberant life.

It was growing dark when I crossed the wall between our street and the ravaged fields behind to gather daisies, purple vetch, buttercups that left their gold dust on my hands and poppies, their black eyes dancing with devilment, shaking out their red skirts and clambering, willy-nilly, over broken blocks and discarded rubble.

The tall grasses brushed my bare legs with silvery fingers and I was back in childhood again, knee deep in the familiar fields of home. I lifted my head once and listened to the distant hum of city traffic, the high, half-frightened laughter of a child. A grasshopper tuned his fiddle absentmindedly and minute insects lifted the note and hummed an old song. A moth rose from beside me and drifted gracefully away, a pale wraith in the gathering darkness.

Dan laughed. '*They saw you coming-seventeen pounds.*' He shook his head, his voice light with love. '*Isn't it a terrible pity now, that a hungry man can't make his dinner out of buttercups?*'

My mother arrived to visit a month later, her blue and white shopping bag crammed with home-made bread and duck eggs and badly knitted cardigans for the baby. Bringing familiarity and reassurance and laughter. Young girl's eyes dancing in the worn lines of her face. I laid the table, taking comfort from the white-gold buttermilk sound of her voice, tartness laced through with small golden globules of laughter. Her shoulders were a little more stooped, the backs of her hands liver spotted, roped with veins. She held the jug held at arm's length- her head on one side, the magpie-light of acquisition deckling her smile.

When she was leaving I wrapped it in towels and yesterday's newspaper. '*Only the loan, mind.*' Her voice, glinting with laughter reassured me, '*You can have it back when I'm gone.*'

She walked away down the path, the shopping bag clutched in her arms like a child. I watched her go with my throat hurting with buried tears of homesickness and loneliness.

I ducked out the back door, away from Dan's exasperated loving bewilderment. I walked through the shrinking flower-meadows behind the little houses, filling my hands with mallow and meadowsweet. The workmen watched with wry kindness and helped me with rough courtesy over cement mixers and broken blocks, the smiles only half-hidden on their sunburned faces.

There was no premonition. I washed up, peeled spuds for the dinner, thinking absent-mindedly of the tall house where I was born. Picturing her walking up the hill with her shopping bag and the house waiting in the quietness, riding the crest of the river road like a gull on a wave.

I slept badly, tossing and turning in the sticky darkness. Woke up exhausted in the half-light of dawn and blacked out ungracefully on the bedroom floor. I opened my eyes to white walls and bright lights and Dan's anxious face.

High blood pressure, they said. Complete rest. The cool professionals with empty eyes and perfectly tailored suits. *'The foetus,'* they murmured among themselves in discreet half-tones, *'the foetus may otherwise be at risk.'*

Stripped to the indignity of a single, perfectly - smoothed sheet with only a chipboard locker separating me from strangers, I lay rigidly, the child quiescent within me. Frightened and bewildered by the deft, probing hands of the custodians of my freedom.

She had been pleased to hear about the child. No wild cries of delight or extravagant showering of kisses. Instead, making bread at the kitchen table, the speckled dough moving under her hands like a living thing, she smiled contentedly at our shared secret.

'Look after yourself,' she said, *'don't be going lifting anything heavy.'*

I smiled in return, chiding her for her old-fashioned daftness. I was young and healthy, pregnancy wasn't an illness,

'I lost four.' Her voice was harsh and I stared at the dough drying on her hands as she held the yellow basin against her breast. *'Four of them. Buried in butter boxes under the apple trees. My lovely little pagans.'* She punched the dough savagely, her voice raw with remembered pain. *'God curse the bloody priests.'*

She put the bowl down softly; there was a white streak of flour on her cross -over apron. The profanity echoed and echoed in the quietness and I sat, shocked into silence, listening to the cat singing himself to sleep in the blue armchair and watched the shadows come creeping from the dim corners of the room and settle on the cold whiteness of her face.

She sighed, kneading the dough round and round the yellow bowl. *'Ah, well, what's past is past, I suppose. Nothing under the apple trees now only nettles and butterflies.'*

She didn't refer to it again. But it was there between us, like a bond, and sometimes, when my child began to flutter in my belly I remembered her lost shadow-children, buried under the apple trees.

In the hushed and harried ward, his face dark with grief and concern, Dan told me of her death. The ward sister stood beside him, ramrod straight in navy blue, her eyes snapping with cold competence. One hand held my wrist, the other, blue-veined, curved around the steel rimmed watch that was pinned to her starched, unmotherly breast.

The lads had found her, Dan said, on their way home from the pub. Half-lying on the grassy ditch outside the haggard gate, her unseeing eyes turned to the buttermilk brightness of the moon.

The ward sister was kind. They all were. Passing in their endless, swift journeyings through the busy wards they smiled vaguely, avoiding my eyes. *'Everything ok Mrs Maher?'*

But never waiting for an answer.

I wanted to go to her funeral. Not advisable, said the consultant gravely, peering through gold-rimmed glasses. Plenty of rest, no unnecessary exertion. Best thing all round.

I turned my back on his spare, grey form and stared at the yellow birds swooping through the willow trees on the curtains around my bed.

I went back to her birthday Mass. My small son snuffling in Dan's arms, wrapped in the blue shawl she'd made him, peering at this strange new world with her wide, grey eyes. The house watched implacably as we climbed the hill, its tall windows staring from its white, unfriendly face.

She was gone. Despite the hiss and crackle of the fire, the clink of glasses, voices raised in greeting, the emptiness ebbed and flowed in the dark corners of familiar rooms. A patch of damp made a map of Italy behind the hall door. A spider crouched by the statue of St. Martin over the fireplace, knitting. Under the stairs, in a carelessly discarded shoe, mice had left a neat pile of shredded paper. I swept it up and tossed it in the fire and found with horror that I could no longer picture her face.

They were gathered in the' good room', the parlour. Grave faces and polite smiles with laughter stifled quickly. My oldest brother, heavy-jowled and stern faced stood backside to the fire, already half-drunk. One hand rested on his wife's thin shoulder. He held a glass in his other hand; the glow of the flames turned the whiskey to a ripple of shot silk. Alice, his wife, sat decorously in the low chair that used to be my mother's, black clad ankles demurely crossed in a perfect parody of royalty. Prim controlled Alice.

Joe, the youngest, leaned against the doorframe, smoking. There was a lost, foolish smile on his unhappy face. And Maurice, the wanderer. Seated in the very centre of the old couch, elegant in pale grey. His body was thin and taut, his face tanned to the point of sallowness. A cut-glass tumbler dangled with careless grace from one slender hand, the other stretched along the back of the seat behind him, his fingers playing absently with a gold pen. His improbable wife, garish and blowsy in green silk, sat a little apart, her eyes bright with sentiment and unshed tears.

I sat in a low chair by the fire, feeling the warmth fingering my face. Firelight flung crazy shadows on the walls and heavy furniture. The faces of our grandparents, sepia brown, smiled and receded into the shadows.

There was waiting on the faces around me. Sideways glances punctuated by uneasy gossip. Everyone talking except Annie and myself. Gypsy-dark Annie, my mother's favourite, staring through the tall windows at the overgrown garden and the bare branches of the apple trees tossing in the wind. I turned to my sleeping son and wished with a sudden gut wrenching sorrow that my mother could have seen him, that I could have heard her white-gold voice tracing likeness and ancestry in his small, unformed face.

I was aware suddenly of the silence that had fallen and the quick, questioning glances between Alice and her husband, the almost imperceptible straightening of her narrow shoulders.

My brother cleared his throat and when he spoke his voice was sombre, with the careful enunciation of the almost-drunk.

'While our dear mother did not leave a written will, she has frequently made it known to Alice and myself that she wished this house and its contents to go to our eldest son, Shaun.' The absurd formality of the words sank into the silence.

There were indrawn breaths of incredulity and anger. Greed, dark and ugly, shadowed familiar faces. Then came the burst of protesting voices and muttered profanities and Alice made the sign of the cross with meticulous piety on her flat, acrylic- clad breast. She glanced at her husband, her hands burrowing like small animals in the folds of her skirt. And, with mounting horror, I heard the ugly, raucous sound of my own voice, cutting through the babble of rage and hostility. The greedy childishness of the words slapping their anger into silence. *'I want my butterfly jug.'*

My brother raised his eyebrows and spoke to me with pitying incredulity. *'That jug may prove to be a valuable part of my son's inheritance.'* And, as if at a signal, Alice reached across and covered my cold hand with both her own.

'After all, dear, we must all respect your dear mother's wishes.'

Annie moved swiftly, reaching into the cupboard in the corner behind her and crossing the room, smiling into my eyes with her hands cupped lovingly around the laughing, beautiful curves of my butterfly jug. Alice turned towards her with a start and the jug fell from Annie's fingers and shattered at my feet. The jagged edges gleaming against the dark lino like newly opened wounds.

I knelt and gathered the pieces in my lap. Blood welled up from a gash on my palm. I held the scarlet - streaked daisies in my cupped palms and heard a woman's voice, high with hysteria and loss. *'They were dancing for her babies. The butterflies were dancing for her babies.'*

Dan helped me to my feet and led me gently away from the averted faces and embarrassed smiles. Their voices murmured understanding and sympathy as I climbed the familiar stairs with my husband's arm around me.

I sat by the window in her room, huddled in the dampness of an old blanket that still retained traces of her smell. Empty.

I could hear the clink of glasses and the comforting rattle of crockery. The parlour door opened once on a wave of angry sound and Alice's voice drifted upwards on the frowsy air, sharp with self-righteous impatience. *'Don't tell me it was shock. Butterflies and dancing babies. The woman is either mad or drunk. If you ask me she's both. But she should have been a bit more careful. That was a very valuable jug.'*

NANCY

Charlotte sat at the kitchen table and thought again the doctors in their starched, white armour and the clinical kindness of their voices that never quite reached their eyes as they told her that there was no more hope for Nancy.

No more hope. She mouthed the words again and then spat them venomously into the quiet and trembled in fury at the memory. Not her Nancy. Beautiful, black haired Nancy with scabby knees and wet kisses and a mouth forever hovering between devilment and tears. Mud on her Sunday shoes and grimy little nails that looked like surprised eyebrows against the scratched pinkness of her hands. Nancy with the laughing face. The song that she had almost forgotten crept into her mind and she had begun to hum it softly to herself while she watched the carefully concealed distaste on their calm, implacable faces.

She switched on the television and the sound of the Angelus reverberated in the warm room, as measured as a gavotte. A calm, blonde newsreader announced the six o'clock news. The funeral had just taken place of a murdered woman whose eleven-year-old son had witnessed the shooting dead of his mother. The Minister of Justice, on behalf of the Government had expressed outrage at the killing. The screen filled with the image of rain falling on shuffling crowds, their eyes slanted slyly towards the cameras in an agony of self-conscious grief.

She watched with distaste with the outpouring of public sorrow, the deference of the crowds as the black-robed priest moved among them with calm, reassuring dignity, his hands raised before him in patronising benediction and his lips moving soundlessly in prayer.

Praying, she thought viciously, praying into the empty silence for a dead mother to a non-existent God.

The cameras homed in lovingly on the face of a child as he stood, open -mouthed and ugly with grief and rain while snot and tears runnelled down his freckled unformed face.

'*Mammy*,' he screamed silently into the warm kitchen, '*Mammy*.'

The image faded again and the newsreader raised her smooth, blonde head and announced smilingly that the Taoiseach was today visiting Brussels for a crucial meeting concerning E.U. funding.

There had been an air-crash in Germany, the girl continued blandly, it was not yet known if there were any survivors. In England a heat wave had brought thousands onto the beaches.

Charlotte rose reluctantly and stretched numbed limbs. In a few minutes her quiet world would explode with the sound of doorbells and the unthinking clamour of young voices. *'How's things Ma? What's for dinner?'* Ruffling the dog's patient head and lifting saucepan lids - avoiding her eyes, ignoring the dark shadows that huddled in hidden corners of the room.

She laid the table precisely and went about the business of preparing the meal with the cold efficiency of an automaton. She chopped herbs and tossed a salad and drained the quietly seething spuds and thought of the child's grief etched against grey stone, as helpless as a butterfly skewered on a pin under the indifferent scrutiny of strangers. She opened the oven and prodded the beef viciously and stirred angry tears into the gravy.

Myeloid leukaemia. Unknown name for an unknown terror. No cure for this evil that had sprung from nowhere and was as familiar now as her own name. The enemy within, striking at Nancy, who was knee-deep in mud and wonder and heedless of the danger. There was nothing to be done, the doctors said, but hope and pray.

She had clung frantically to that hope, grabbing gratefully at the Mass cards and blessed rosaries and bits of improbably white cloth reputedly cut from the robes of long dead saints that were offered to her by moist-eyed neighbours. Listened courteously as they repeated over and over the mantra of God's will, God's holy will, her mind screaming at them to fuck off, just fuck off and mind their own fucking, morbid, blood-sucking business. Smiling and in control and mouthing obscenities at their mistily smiling faces in her mind.

Casting around in her mind for somebody to blame. Farmers, diesel fumes, food additives, God, as Nancy shrivelled in the high hospital bed while the harsh neon painted grey shadows on the unfinished perfection of her eight-year-old face.

She hadn't prayed in years but weeks ago, while there was still some hope to cling to, she had begun to attend church regularly again, kneeling beside Josh, her husband, while the twins and Jodie lit rows of candles before the smiling gaze of a marble, blank faced virgin. She wore bright clothes and painted her nails the pale pink of the inside of a shell and raged silently at the false anguish of an uncaring world as she sat by Nancy's bed and smoothed endlessly the nubbly white bedspread.

Reading over and over again the plethora of cards on the steel-framed window ledge. *Get Well Soon* and *Thinking of You* and *God Bless.* Fluffy rabbits and a doll's hat trimmed with daisies and a morose Christ with nail-pierced, outstretched hands. Blank faced plastic statues of the Virgin filled with holy water and on the foot-rail a red clipboard with a single sheet of paper that traced Nancy's journey to the grave.

On Tuesday, at ten past three in the afternoon, Nancy died. By nightfall the house was crowded with people. They reminded her of rats, grey rats that crowded around her and thanked God for the swiftness of her child's death and marvelled at the mercy of a Deity who had saved Nancy from further pain. She stood with her head bowed and cursed them silently while she felt the cold press of their unknown fingers on her hands and her shoulders and her face. What about my pain, my fucking, fucking, curse of God fucking whoring pain-as if the profanities were some magic incantation that could erase by their very crudeness the terrible certainty of her loss.

They thronged through her house and drank tea or whiskey and crowded into the blue and white bedroom and whispered in sibilant awe at the still beauty of Nancy lying in her yellow dress, her dark hair tumbled on a starched white pillow. Look at her, they murmured, wouldn't you think she was asleep? A little angel, they sighed, safe with Jesus, playing with the angels. They sipped tea from a neighbour's china cups as she walked dreamlike through rooms lit with candlelight and joined in long, droning rosaries and thanked them endlessly for their gifts of flowers and tears and apple cake and offer of spare beds for the relations and her mouth ached from the effort of smiling. She smiled and accepted their gifts politely, certain that it was all a huge con trick perpetuated by the priests, those spin-doctors of heaven and the world to come. We'll meet again and the circle will not be broken and resurrection of the body and life everlasting amen. Lies, all of it. There was no more Nancy. Nothing but a white shell to be washed and ringleted and wept over and dressed in a yellow dress.

At Nancy's funeral she sat, straight-backed and rigid and watched the mourners from behind the secure shelter of her rage. Marvelling to herself as she saw the shaky sophistication of eighteen stripped effortlessly away as the twins moaned softly into their cupped hands. She counted the freckles that stood out, bright as pennies, on Jodie's little face. Her husband clutched her arm, his fingers digging painfully into her flesh, and she flinched and withdrew from him and listened with mild, impatient distaste to the sobbing of those around her and flowery sentimentality of the priest who spoke so movingly of the child he had never known. The Communion bell sounded and somewhere at the back of the church a young girl began to sing and the congregation rose and began to file towards the altar and returned with reverently folded hands, touching her shoulder lightly as they passed. She emptied her eyes and folded her mouth sternly against their watching and swore that she would not become some grief-ravaged image in their mind's -eye, a peep show of sorrow for family and friends, all these lovely, kind people, these tragedy-hungry hordes.

She closed her eyes against all of it -the garish brightness of flowers and the ineffectual flicker of the tall white candles and anger roared through her for the remembered face of the little snot-nosed star of the six o'clock news.

She walked away from Nancy's grave and found that her mind had become a labyrinth of empty rooms to which she could open and close the doors at will. Suffering and grief was a simple issue of mind over matter. Clichéd wisdom gleaned from newspapers, television, old magazine articles, drifting through her mind. There are no victims, only volunteers.

She gloried in her own strength, secretly contemptuous of the weakness of others. She was no-one's volunteer, no-one's victim; the obscenity of Nancy's going would not destroy her.

She listened to her husband's grieving and wanted to shake him from his self-pitying stupor but found herself drowning in apathy instead. Unsolicited literature came through her letterbox in a deluge of sentimental rubbish. She opened one or two of the offerings and threw the rest away, unread. Cold-eyed, she watched her children's frantic search for a stop-gap for their terror and closed her mind to their futile whistling in the dark.

September came and the twins returned to school and Jodie got a new bike for his birthday. Nancy was a grief that would fade into a wraith that would one day dissolve into the mundanity of everyday things. She was locked in a room in Charlotte's mind where she steadfastly refused to go.

She filled her mind instead with images of the small boy weeping on the television screen until gradually her obsession grew as she cringed at her own indifference to the vulnerability of his grief. Her nights were filled with dreams in which she drifted down a long corridor with glass walls while ahead of her the boy fled, sobbing. She called to him but when he turned to her there were only shadows in the empty sockets of his eyes. She'd wake screaming and her husband held her against him and murmured inanities in her ear, rocking her against him as if she was a child, his own tears wet against her face.

When morning came she comforted herself with the conviction that somehow she would find the child and share her knowledge and her strength with him, teach him how to build bulwarks against a world grown vociferous for the sight of suffering and pain.

She searched for him everywhere, caught glimpses of his half-remembered face at school football matches or speeding on roller skates along city pavements. She'd come face to face with some freckled youngster outside a cinema or in the park and would search his face for signs of grief and raging silently to herself as the child ducked his head uneasily to avoid the pity in her eyes, the unease sometimes turning to fear as she caught his arm, trying passionately to find the words to tell him that she meant no harm, she wished only to return to him his dignity and repair the damage caused by the unthinking voyeurism of an indifferent world.

The days shortened and she took to walking in the woods, finding an uneasy peace in the yielding moist darkness of moss and dead leaves and the arrogant, rigid sureness of the trees. She took an almost sensual pleasure in the musty warmth of clothes damp and pungent with rain.

She met him at last, as she had known she would, under the shelter of stand of silver birch, stripped bare by November wind. He was riding a bicycle, blue and silver, the wheels twisted tortuously on the muddied track.

She smiled in recognition and relief at the sight of his freckled face and still faintly red-rimmed eyes. She held her hands out and he stopped with a muddy flourish, straddling the bike with stiff-legged arrogance as she strove at last to voice her gratitude at having found him. The words tumbling from her in an agony of relief and regret until at last she fell silent, aghast at the sneering indifference on his face and the inane gabble of her own voice dribbling into the silence.

He dismounted without speaking and dropped the bike carelessly on the side of the path, holding her effortlessly with the flat menace of his eyes. He was older and bigger than she remembered from the television screen. She noticed that he had dirty teeth, small pustules dotted his face. He walked towards her, forcing her back into the shadowy undergrowth, matching her steps like a dancer.

Terror kicked her finally in the gut and she tried to push past, forcing her face into a grimace of outraged anger but he shoved at her shoulder peevishly, like a child anxious to start a quarrel with a playmate.

He began to unhook his belt, smiling slowly to himself, and beyond her fear she could see the shadows of a million cowboy heroes in the swagger of his hips. He dropped the belt at her feet and thrust out a booted foot and she sprawled at his feet and lay helplessly watching as his thumbs eased his jeans past his hips in the slow-motion parody of a striptease. His belly was white, scribbled over with coarse reddish hairs.

'*Lie down.*' His voice was low, the edges cracking into manhood. He poked at her shoulder indifferently with his foot, as if she was an insect or a wounded animal. And terrified at last, she read the insolence and careless lust on his froglike, loose-lipped face.

She rolled suddenly, curled like an animal, and kicked out with the strength of her terror. He fell awkwardly and she heard the sickening crack of bone and lashed out again, her body pulsing with rage. Her shoe caught him on the jaw and she felt a rush of vicious pleasure at the sound of the thud of leather on bone. His face crumpled and he began to whimper softly to himself, knuckling his eyes like a child.

She stood over him, invincible in her fury and turned away from his fear, giving a last contemptuous kick towards his bloodied chin. She could smell the acrid smell of stale sweat and the appled tang of cheap cider and noticed for the first time the scatter of red-gold hairs that gleamed uneasily on his pimpled chin.

She walked away without looking back and felt her body settle into tranquillity as she thought of all the tears, all the grief and loving remembrance that she had stolen from Nancy. And deep inside she felt the first faint glitch of pain.

She would go home, she decided, and smile at Jodie and pour a drink for herself and Mike and make rock buns for the tea. And sprinkling the sugar she would remark, quite casually, *'remember how she always wanted to help with this bit and get most of the sugar on the floor, she always managed to make such a mess.'*

And Jodie would giggle and the twins might smile, remembering, and then she would change the subject so that the moment might be quickly over.

Tomorrow, though. Tomorrow she would begin to cry for Nancy.

THE OTHER SIDE OF NOWHERE

'Mamsie?'

'Nella?'

'Hello? You still there, Mamsie? It's me, Nella. I'm home.'

'Mamsie' Your name for me while you were still learning to talk. Before Mamsie became Mammy and then 'Ma' - a peevish, accusatory, retort that ended every argument between us even before it had even begun.

People disappear all the time. A woman writes a shopping list, walks down her garden path and nods good morning to a passing neighbour. She is never seen again. Someone steps off a bus in a quite village on a summer evening. Years later, a man walking on a mountain or fishing for trout on the shore of some remote lake discovers a handful of bleached bones.

I remember the Gardaí arriving, sometime about daybreak. They stood in the hallway, avoiding my eyes, slapping rubber torches against their black -gloved hands.

A sign that read **KEEP OUT** hung on your bedroom door. The red mini-skirt that caused that last, terrible row with your father was flung across a chair where you had thrown it in petulant, childish rage. I found myself apologising as I picked up knickers and stray socks from the cluttered, unhoovered floor. My ears straining for the sound of a footstep, the click of the garden gate, as I furtively wiped dust from the dressing table with the sleeve of my new Christmas dress.

The sergeant sat at the kitchen table, noting your height, hair colour, the clothes you were wearing, on a page of a tattered notepad with random phone numbers scribbled on the cover.

His big, raw-knuckled hands awkwardly holding a cheap, plastic pen.

You made the headlines that evening, your disappearance flashed around the country on radio and television news.

'When last seen she was wearing ...'

Images of your school friends filled the screen, looked shy and self-important as they jostled each other for space in front of the cameras.

'Anyone with any information is asked to contact the Gardaí.'

Neighbours called, bringing Mass cards, flowers, apple tarts with singed and blackened edges, ham sandwiches that wilted in the heat of the overcrowded kitchen, curling at the edges like the collar of a badly ironed blouse.

I remember the nights when I fought against sleep and nodded in a chair by the telephone knowing that you were waiting to come dancing out of subconscious darkness to torment me with your gap-toothed, secretive smile. Not your fifteen-year-old self with your defiant, painted eyes and bony little face, but as a small girl of six or seven with your front teeth missing and ribbons in your curls.

We were still clinging to hope then, on those merciless mornings when your father came home from trawling the city streets and stood in the doorway with the milk bottles cradled against his chest.

Shaking his head.

The skin stretched tight across his bones.

One heart -stopping morning the phone rang towards dawn and a woman -sounding hesitant and frightened- asked to speak to Dominic. Wrong number, I said, and she put the phone down with an angry click. Then the other calls began. Silence this time, or the sound of smothered laughter. Someone's idea of a joke, the Guards said. A lot of sick people out there.

We took down the Christmas tree. The school re-opened and held a special Mass for your safe return. Tulips bloomed in the garden. The days lengthened into a cold, damp summer. Women walked dogs in the thin, watery sunlight, wearing baggy, ill-fitting shorts over goose-pimpled thighs. Your schoolmates, giddy as spring lambs, celebrated the Junior Cert results. Some of them got drunk and threw up cheap cider and curry on pavements or over garden walls.

You were gone nearly two years when a therapist, a grey haired woman with tired eyes and a lined, unfriendly face advised us to give up our search. We must learn to let go and accept and acknowledge our loss. Acceptance would bring closure.

The words flowed easily from her. Her well-used mantras.

Closure.

Such a meaningless, ridiculous word.

And still I clung frantically to the last vestiges of hope. And when hope finally died, I turned to the tarot readers, spiritualists, shamans, mystics, sons of seventh sons. The gypsy dealt her cards: the Chariot, the Wheel of Fortune, The Tower, The Hanging Man, the Sun, The Moon, The Star, on a table covered with a crimson velvet cloth. She held my hand between warm, calloused fingers as she murmured her singsong, well - worn promises of old loves and new loves and journeys and great good fortune still to come. Reading the shadows under my eyes, the paler skin on my ring finger where the mark of my wedding ring was still indented.

But the dark eyed gypsy found no trace of you in the silvery depths of her pretty crystal ball. The ectoplasmic ghosts gave up none of your secrets. Not one of the wise women or the charlatans even guessed that you were gone.

On the evening of you eighteenth birthday I went outside and carefully, with pegs and string, measured a plot of ground under the cherry tree. Six feet by three. It was dark by the time I'd finished, a sullen overcast night with no stars.

Your father stood at the back door, shaking his head.

'I give up,' he said. *'This is the limit. I give up.'*

He went back inside again to the lighted kitchen and closed the door behind him.

It took me nearly a week to dig a shallow trench, shivering in the October rain. And when it was finished, I gathered up your childhood dolls and storybooks and teddy bears. The garnet ring we gave you on your Confirmation Day. Your new daisy -printed pyjamas, your pound shop jewellery and old Valentine's cards and school uniform with the hated lace-up shoes. I buried them all and planted the soil over them with flowers whose names you loved.

Bear's Ear and Lady's Fingers.

Creeping Jenny and Glory of the Snow.

It must be seven or eight years ago now since I caught sight of you crossing the Ha'penny Bridge. You were with a man, youngish, foreign –looking, with dark, slicked back hair and a sallow, Eastern European face. I'd have known you anywhere-the swing of your hips, the way you flicked your hair out of your eyes as you walked. I ran after you, full of rage at the callous way he held you trapped against him with his fingers curled roughly around your arm, just above the elbow. But when I got close enough I saw that it wasn't you after all. This woman was older, her hair coarse and lustreless, already greying. She was speaking to her companion in a language I didn't understand.

You haunted me for years. Once I turned my head and caught the pale outline of your face etched against the window of a passing bus. On Stephen's Green, a laugh that sounded just like yours rose from a tangle of students sprawled on the scuffed, litter-strewn grass. When the television cameras panned the crowds in Croke Park or Lansdowne Road or the Galway Races, I caught a glimpse of you waving your flag, cheering the winners on, jumping up and down with delight.

But I stopped searching for you long ago, Nella.

I haven't dreamed about you in years.

Now I have different dreams. I sit in a small boat, in the middle of a river that is hardly more than a stream, while others travel past me at great speed as I spin helplessly round and round, caught in the whirlpool of their passing.

I'm still here, in the house where you were born. I work as a housekeeper for a retired priest. I have settled for the banality of peace, the monotony of structured days. Father Jude is a solitary man. A scholar. He once told me that he cherishes the freedom of silence.

He is a truly good priest.

He has never burdened me with hope.

Your father lives in Killiney now with your new stepmother; rich, brisk, sensible Kate. I visited their house once when his mother – your Grandma Annie - died. Kate believes in being civilised. She offered me tea and, when I refused, she walked me to the gate, down a pale, gravelled path, past birdbaths and fountains of polished stone. Kate has better things to do with her life than stare out the kitchen window at flowers growing on an imitation grave.

'Mamsie?'

This is no dream. Your voice in my ear is real enough, although it sounds tinny and very far away .But the soothsayers and spiritualists taught me that reality is not to be trusted. This could be just another cruel and callous hoax. Or I think of brain haemorrhage or stroke as I reach out for comfort and touch the carved headboard that once belonged to my mother. My feet, in scuffed slippers, rest easily on this familiar carpet with its pattern of faded roses. I count the mundane objects on my bedside table; three library books, a bedside lamp, tissues. An alarm clock and an empty glass. Your picture- the only one of you I possess- hangs in a silver frame above my bed. It was taken the Christmas you went away. You were smiling, holding a bunch of grapes over your head, pretending it was mistletoe.

> Sweat beads my forehead and runs down my face like fat, acrid tears.
>
> The thin morning sunlight streaming through the window splinters into jagged shards of brightness.
>
> The room is going black.
>
> I have no breath left in me.
>
> The bones of my legs are dissolving.
>
> I am seeping into the carpet's pale pink roses.

When I come back to consciousness, I am lying on the floor with the phone dangling beside me. You smile down at me from your silver frame with your fifteen-year-old mouth pouted flirtatiously for a kiss.

This morning you just walked into a Garda station in Kinsale and asked the desk sergeant to contact your father. Now he holds me in an exuberant, awkward embrace, his face incandescent with delight. He has organised a taxi directly from Cork to take you straight home before the media finds out and all hell breaks loose.

'*A miracle-an absolute miracle,*' he says, over and over again.

'*All these years she was in Glasgow - an hour or two away by plane. Why couldn't she let us know? All these years.*'

Neither of us knows how to answer. We sit side by side at the kitchen table, drinking brandy at eleven o'clock in the morning. His fingers holding the glass have grown soft and womanly, with polished, manicured nails. But his hair is greyer now- when he bends his head a bald spot is clearly visible, with the scalp shining pinkly through.

So-here you are at last. You are taller than I remember. In the eleven years since you've been gone, your body has renewed itself, cell by cell, until you have become a stranger.

A woman grown.

You toss a denim jacket carelessly on an armchair. Your shoulders and arms are tattooed with the Rose and Thistle of Scotland, the name Ian, a bluebird with a black, beady eye.

You catch my eye and shrug and smile. Your voice has a soft, unfamiliar burr.

'*A moment of madness,*' you say. '*It's good to be home.*'

There are no happy endings, Nella. When I hold you your body feels hard and unyielding in my embrace. In these long years since your going, your father has borne his burden bravely, like a soldier carrying the hidden wounds of war. I watch you lean into him like a triumphant lover as he weeps and wraps his arms around you and smiles at you with gentle, forgiving eyes.

But I am learning, too late, that my ephemeral and hard -won serenity is built on rubble of bones.

THE WAR ISN'T OVER YET

'Bloody foreigners,' said my father, the soldier. *'We gave Jerry what for, we did. Hitler didn't know what bloody hit him.'*

Every Christmas it was the same. He'd listen to the Queen's speech on the wireless with the weight of his war medals pulling peevishly at the shabby lapels of his good suit, and afterwards drink her Majesty's health with maudlin patriotism, raising his bottle of brown ale to the proud, remote profile that hung over the fireplace.

'Her Majesty, God bless her.'

And the heels of his shoes would click together like the closing of a trap.

When I told him that Donal was Irish he looked at me for a long moment, and then turned and left the room with speaking. We could hear his muttered curses as he climbed the stairs. When he came down again, he held his war medals in his clenched fist, the heavy ribbons bright against the knotted veins of his hands. He flung them at my feet.

'Dance on them why don't you?'

'I'm marrying him,' I said. *'I'm marrying Donal.'*

He turned from me, the blood creeping up and turning the network of lines at the back of his neck into a spider's web of rage.

'You listening Mum?' he crowed, *'our daughter, the child and grandchild of soldiers, is marrying a Paddy.'*

She put the potato she was peeling carefully down on the sink and turned towards me, her eyes frantic with pleading. He thrust his face close to mine and I could smell the sour, old man smell of him and the pungent whiff of ale.

'We're not having it,' he shouted. *'You ain't marrying no bloody Paddy. Right Mum?'* Small gobbits of spit flew from his lips and landed wetly on my face.

She nodded mutely and I could see her shoulders stretched and taut under her thin blouse, like a kite braced against the wind.

He watched me slyly for a minute, the thin lines of his face folded into malice.

'You're not in the pudding club, I hope?'

'No,' I said. *'Nothing like that.'* I was watching my mother's face.

He laughed coarsely and she made a small, protesting sound deep in her throat as he flung himself into a chair. Incongruously he began to hum. 'Keep the home fires burning', his fingers tapping a dead-march accompaniment on chair's wooden arm.

'Can't say I'm surprised,' he said at last. *'Your granddad was over in 1919 –gave the bloody Irish what for, he did. Bloody priest- ridden savages, the lot of them.'*

He stood up and went to my mother and laid a hand on her arm and she flinched at his touch.

'Don't you worry none, Mum,' he said, *'Our Jillie can tell them all about her granddad who did his duty for King and Country.'* He turned and spat into the fireplace and the spittle hissed malevolently against the hot coals. *'Welcome our girl with open arms–they will. Very hospitable people –the bloody Irish.'*

'It's not like that anymore,' I shouted at his retreating back. *'That was forty years ago. People are different now. You have to let the past go. Even you can't fight forever.'*

He turned to look at me over a shoulder rimed with dandruff-there was a sad bitterness in his eyes.

'*You do what you want,*' he said, '*but the war, it ain't over yet.*'

Donal laughed, his black curls were sleek as a seal's with the rain. He slit a cigarette wrapper with his thumbnail and I watched the lighted match as it blackened and bent and a small tongue of flame licked viciously at his fingers. He cursed softly as he dropped the spent match carelessly at his feet.

He hit the table with his fist and beer ran from his glass and sloshed across the speckled Formica like a small, muddy river.

His mother wrote. He showed me her letter, sitting on the edge of an unmade bed in a cramped bed-sitter in Cricklewood. The words were stiff and formal, straggling off the page in a mess of violet ink. His father wasn't well, she wrote, maybe Donal should be thinking of coming home and taking his place on the land. She was glad he had met a nice girl –for all that she was English. She enclosed a relic of St. Martin for me and sent her best regards. She would be praying for her son and hoping that he would do nothing foolish.

I put the little picture in my handbag, trying to hide my distaste. '*You didn't tell her I wasn't a Catholic.*'

My voice sounded accusing.

'*Hush,*' he said. He was laughing. '*You could be a bare-arsed heathen for all I care.*'

He pulled me back against the frowsy sheets and I watched his eyes grow heavy as he wrapped me in his nakedness and together we hung, spread-eagled on the rim of the world.

His mother wrote again a month later. His father was worse, she said, he was wanted at home. He buried his brown face in my neck and begged me to marry him. He wouldn't go home without me.

We were married in a registry office. There were no guests but my mother and a sad looking clerk. My father refused to come. It rained and the drops slid listlessly down the tall windows, tracing little silver highways in the dust. Donal looked ill at ease in a new suit. My mother cried softly and the registrar coughed continually, the sound rattling like loose gravel in his chest. The gold band felt heavy and awkward on my finger.

Outside on the pavement we stood in an awkward huddle. My mother kissed me, embraced Donal awkwardly. *'You'll write,'* she pleaded, unshed tears flickering behind her eyes. *'Promise me you'll write.'*

We went home to Kerry that night. It was cold on the ship's deck, the damp spray burrowing into my bones. I sat in the bar for a while It was crowded with returning emigrants. Young men like Donal, with strong, sunburned faces, old men with sad eyes and rough, scarred hands. They sang, maudlin sentimental songs, their eyes full of drunken tears,

Donal slouched against the bar, his arm heavy across my shoulders. His eyes were shadowed and wary. I sat watching his brown throat rippling as he swallowed long draughts of beer, the cold saltiness of the sea in my mouth. My wedding ring was a dull glint in the smoke-filled room. Donal, sullen and heavy-eyed, watched me, his face closed against me.

I went outside in the end, driven by the smoke and the casual profanities and the heavy weight of my husband's arm across my tired shoulders. My husband, I said silently watching the waves lick the sides of the ship like eager lovers. My husband. I tasted the warm curves of the sound on my tongue. A young man staggered towards me and sagged against the railing in pool of his own vomit. He was crying, the high-pitched wail of a child. Below in the bar someone was singing Moonlight in Mayo.

The train was cold and damp and Donal slept, his body huddled against me. I lay against the window, cradling him with my arm, grateful for his warmth. He roused once. Joe, he mumbled, Joe would meet us at the station. Good old Joe.

It was almost night when the train shuddered into the small station. I stood up and smoothed down the skirt of my wedding dress, tried to stretch cramped and frozen limbs. Donal looked ill, his face green in the light of the station lamps.

Joe was there. Big and broad and red-faced. He was the local hackney, he told me cheerfully, hooking Donald's arm expertly across his shoulder. *'You'll be the English bride, so,'* he asked. *'That's right,'* I said, *'You must excuse Donal-it's been a long day. He's just tired.'*

He laughed a deep rich laugh that rumbled up from his belly.

'You don't have to tell me,' he said, *'It's not the first time I've seen this boy tired.'* He slapped Donal roughly on the shoulder. *'Wake up Donal, the whole parish is above in the house waiting to see the bride.'*

Donal stirred and groaned.

'Jesus, Joe, I think I left my head on the fuckin' boat.'

The house was at the end of a laneway, gleaming quietly against the darkness of the mountains. The door was open, light spilled on cobbles. A tall woman stood in the doorway, her face in shadow. Donal fumbled with the car door handle, cursing softly, and fell into her waiting arms. Her hands with their blackened nails held him fiercely against her and I heard the pride and defiance in his voice,

'Mam, this is Jillie.'

She watched me, not moving and my outstretched hand hung foolishly in the silence between us. *'Your father is below in the byre,'* she said at last. *'I've put you in the small room beyond.'*

I found the nightly ritual of the Rosary strange and disturbing. The realisation that I was not a Catholic had come to them slowly .I watched the taciturn old man that was Donal's father fall painfully to his knees, kissing the cross at the his beads on the end with fervour. My Protestant soul cringed from such idolatry.

It came to me slowly that I was expected to make this house my home. I looked at Donal, disbelieving. *'I can't leave,'* he said, *'If I go now he might leave the land to one of the sisters instead.'*

'It's too small,' I protested. *'And what about your mother. What happens to her?'*

His face flushed with the darkness of anger.

'For fucks sake-you'd think you were born in Buckingham Palace. Isn't it as good and better than what you were used to?'

I hated the small, smoky rooms. Holy pictures and plastic statues watched me accusingly from every shelf. I grew to loathe the brown paint that was smeared, thick as butter, on the kitchen door, the thin-lipped forbidding sepia photograph of De Valera as he looked with cold disapproval at St. Patrick treading snakes into the top of the dresser. There was no noise but the news on the wireless, the lowing of animals and the bad-tempered barking of the farm dogs. I sat at night and watched the neighbour's playing cards and listened to the sound of their voices making alien music of my language.

His mother doled out small kindnesses. She taught me how to bake. *'Jillie,'* she said, holding the strangeness of the word on her tongue. *'You were named for your mother, maybe?'*

'No,' I said, *'She got the name out of a library book.'*

Her eyes were pitying. *'It's a strange way of naming a child. In this country we name our children to renew the dead.'*

My mother wrote seldom. Her letters seemed to come from another world. She said my father sent his regards. I didn't believe her. My own letters were filled with lies and half-truths. I didn't mention my father. I didn't want to care.

They began going to the pub every night, Donal and his father. He would look at me, his dark eyes defiant. *'We'll go down to Joe Dan's for an hour'* and the look on his mother's face stilled the protests on my mouth. *'Let them be,'* she said, *'the men are entitled.'*

When I put my coat on, ready to go with them she stood in the doorway, barring me, her face rigid with shock. *'Sweet Holy Jesus,'* she said her eyes bright with anger and distress.

'Do you want to be the talk of the parish? Isn't it enough that you won't turn to the one true God?'

The priest visited and she left us alone together in the front room. She brought Marie biscuits and sherry in delicate, dusty glasses.

I tried to explain to him about my lack of faith in any particular God. My casual Church of England upbringing wouldn't stretch to his rituals and ceremonies and prayers. He smiled patiently as if I were a wayward child.

'It will come,' he promised, his thumbs meeting in smug accord across his broad, black-clad chest. 'This is a good Catholic home. I'll get the sodality to do the Nine Fridays for you. The Sacred Heart won't refuse the prayer of a mother.'

I smiled and nodded. But I didn't understand.

I sat for a long time after he'd gone, drowning in rage and self-pitying loneliness. When I went down to the kitchen she smiled at me.

'You'll be hungry so, after your long chat,' she said. 'I'll make a few pancakes for the supper.'

Nancy, who was married to Donal's cousin, called to the house most weeks. She was cheerful and broad hipped, gap-toothed like a schoolboy. She had seven children. 'Isn't it well to be you,' she'd say, 'and you as slim as a willow wand.' Her voice laughing and her eyes flickering over the flatness of my belly and the barely visible swell of my breasts.

I thought a child might change things, might bring back the light to Donal's eyes. Night after night I lay in the small room and listened for the sounds of his homecoming. Always the same. Smothered laughter and the clatter of bicycles thrown carelessly against the byre wall, heavy footsteps and muttered goodnights to his father and the weight of his body trapping me against the thin mattress in the whiskey –smelling dark.

Afterwards, just before we drifted into sleep, I'd plead for a place of our own. He'd lean over and take me by the shoulders, butting me against the pillows with careful savagery. 'Do you never give up?'

The laughter gathering in his voice as he pulled me against him.

'Come here,' he said, 'come here and make me a son.'

It took three years of despair and hope and avoiding the eternal question in his mother's eyes. The doctor was old, smelling of peppermints and tobacco. He knew who I was without asking.

'Good news,' he said smiling. *'Donal waited a long time for this.'*

'I waited too,' I said. *'I waited the longest.'*

I cycled home slowly, thinking of the child growing inside me who would one day walk and cycle along these quiet roads. His hair black like Donal's, his curls slicked back with water, sleek as the head of a young seal. Going down of a night to Joe Dan's with Donal, his father.

'Make me a son.' he had said, *'make me a son.'*

She was in the kitchen, baking. She stood with her back to me.

'You just missed Nancy,' she said, *'she had a bit of news for us. She's expecting again in the harvest.'*

She slapped the bread into the tin, two bright spots of anger on her cheeks. Her face was cold.

'Eight sons and daughters for Nancy,' she said,' *and you as barren as an old woman still.'*

Tears sparkled at the corners of her eyes.

'Maybe if you came down off your high horse and was baptised like a Christian, God wouldn't be turning his face away from my son.' She spat the words at me.

'My father was right. There never was anything but bad luck from the bloody English.'

I went outside and leaned against the wall. I fell sick and cold. In a few moments she followed me and now her voice was soft, trembling on the edge of tears.

She laid her hand on my arm.

'I'm sorry,' she said.' *I had no call to say what I did. I just thought you might have brought some news from the town.'*

I smiled at her. *'No news,'* I said. *'It's all right, we all make mistakes.'*

I went down to the little room where we slept and sat on the end of the bed with my arms wrapped around myself for comfort. I thought of the sounds of his homecoming, the laughter and the clatter of the bike flung carelessly against the wall. Nancy's eyes on the small mound of my belly under the crossover apron.

By the time they came back from Joe Dan's I was gone.

WHISTLING IN THE DARK

Chrissie was on holiday in Morocco when the telegram came. 'Regret to inform you of death of your father, John Boyle,' it stated baldly, 'Funeral Monday at ten, internment immediately afterwards.'

Signed, not by her mother, but by the parish priest.

That night she lay awake for a long time remembering the dour, cold-faced man who had been her father. The words of the telegram jostling behind her closed eyelids as she willed her mind to give them substance. But they swooped around in her head, a meaningless mantra, as irrelevant as an old shopping bill.

She slept fitfully and dreamed of childhood Sundays, of coming in from First Mass, the Sunday Press, Flip and Casey, Dagwood and Blondie, Michael O'Hehir on the Pye wireless, the brash beauty of a brass band, Father thumping the table *kick the ball, ye blind hoor* the exuberance of the commentator's voice echoing and rebounding in the foetid little room, shouts of unseen people, the green eye of the wireless blinking from the smoky dimness of the shelf over the fire like a sleepy cat, the click, click, click of Mammy's knitting needles and the passionate roar of ten thousand voices singing 'The Rose of Tralee.'

Her husband Walter, his kind face creased in concern, was insistent on accompanying her, despite the frailty of his health. In the end they compromised-she would take Gerry, her son, instead.

They hired a car in Dublin Airport and drove through drowsing Saturday morning suburbs while Chrissie leaned her head wearily against the headrest and watched the clock on the dashboard glowering in silent accusation.

'Can't you go any faster?' Her breath shivered on an angry sob and he patted her knee absently, as if she were a child.

'Relax, Mum, we can't possibly make it in time now anyway. Try and get some rest while you can.'

Smiling at her with the lovely, heart-stopping smile of his father.

Presently she slept and dreamed of dark, smiling faces under the harsh glare of the Moroccan sun.

'You're done with the schooling now Miss,' her father announced suddenly, the year she turned thirteen.

'You have enough book –learning, there's hay to be reared, turf to be cut. Your mother will be wanting help around the house.'

Her mother said nothing, gathering up the buckets for milking and slipping out the door like an apologetic shadow.

She was sixteen when she told him she wanted to look for a job in the town. He was in rare good humour, the weather had held out until the last of the hay was safely in the shed and the turf clamped in black huddles against the byre wall.

'The hotel is looking for a girl for the kitchen. I'm sixteen now. I could go in on the bicycle.'

Her voice high-pitched, the words strangling in her throat.

Her mother kneaded bread silently, her bent head a dark etching against the little window and Father pared tobacco, rubbing the dark, pungent slivers in the palm of his hand.

He spat into the ashes.

'There'll be no hotel. Haven't you enough to be doing at home?'

'Yes Father.'

She'd always called him 'Father'.

And so she stayed, lost in the colourless monotony of days that were lived out of sight and sound of the world around her. Smothered between Mammy's anxious, elderly love and Father's barely concealed contempt for both of them because he had no son to win him back the two lovely fields that were stolen from his grandfather by the Soraghans when the poor man wasn't in his right mind, and all for the price of a gallon of porter.

And night after Summer night, when the evening Rosary had been said, she'd lie sleepless in the half-darkness beside her opened window and listen to the music from the dancehall in the town come drifting over the hayshed to shake the heart out of her with its sweetness .

Gerry stopped at a pub where a hand-painted sign offering refreshments swayed with brisk self-importance above a blue- painted door. He ordered hot whiskey and she warmed her hands gratefully on the glass and then drank quickly, gagging at the pungent sweetness. In the cloakroom, at the end of a passage that stank of urine and stale vomit, she stared at her pale, frightened reflection as she washed her hands in a doll-sized sink clinging grimly to the wall under a mirror that was cracked and mottled with age.

Father let her go to her first dance when she was just nineteen. She got a lift with neighbours. The lads she'd known from schooldays gathered in graceless huddles under the stage and ignored her, sniggering and jostling each other like unruly children. She danced with ageing bachelors who splayed hot fingers against her buttocks, pressing her unwilling body slyly against them and she burned with shame in the stiff, gold brocade that had come in a parcel from America when her mother was still a child. Old school friends brushed past her, girls with pale mouths and tight jumpers outlining the smug neatness of their dainty little breasts.

'Gorgeous dress, Chrissie. You're making a pure show of the rest of us.'

The spiteful ripple of their laughter almost bringing her to tears. Until Aiden O'Halloran, slouched against the grimy walls like a graceful shadow, raised a hand in careless greeting and smiled at her with his dark-lashed, beautiful eyes.

He stubbed out his cigarette with the heel of his dusty shoe and caught her lazily against him and whirled her away under the fly-speckled bulbs while the band played **'China Doll'**.

Every night, all through that hot and humid summer she waited, taut as a bowstring, listening for the low, piercing thrill of a blackbird that was his signal. And at the sound, she was down the lane and tumbling into his arms in the scented softness of the ditch. His hands a warm sweetness on her skin as he whispered his promises of Australia, America, Canada - the wide world that waited for them beyond the scrubby hedges that bounded her father's sour, little fields.

Letting herself be bound and entrapped in the spiders -web of his dreams.

'*I got you now,*' Father crowed. ' *I've snared my lovely cock blackbird at last.*'

He dragged Chrissie half-naked and weeping, from the ditch and drove her up the lane before him, hitting her lightly on the shoulders with a switch of hazel, as if she were a cow. He forbade her to leave the house, not even to go to Mass. On the fifteenth of August he went to the Scrabby Fair and came home drunk, with the news that Aiden O'Halloran was gone to Alaska that very morning to search for Yukon gold.

The next day she woke to the sound of the dull thud of Father's fist on the kitchen table, and her own name being shouted, and finally, the sound of a door being slammed and her mother moaning, '*Ah, no John no, John.*'

Her voice sodden with weeping.

Father and Jamsie Soraghan, old enmities forgotten, came swaying up the lane together at nightfall with entwined arms and mouths viscous with dark slobbers of porter.

She felt the drunken sting of Father's slap on her backside as she turned salt rashers in the pan with a blackened fork.

'*Isn't she a fine girl, Jamsie? The finest girl in the seven parishes.*'

He rubbed his hands gleefully between his knees like a child nursing a secret.

Next morning, milking the black heifer, with her face resting against the animal's silky flank, she listened as Father told her she was to marry Jamsie Soraghan. A fine fresh man, not yet sixty, and there wasn't one in the whole of Ireland that could point the finger and say she was walking land that wasn't hers by right.

The two high fields were coming back to them that rightfully owned them at last.

His voice rising against her silence and the milk lashing against the side of the bucket with the sound of tearing silk.

She slid out of bed in the false dawn and crept down the stairs, listening to his drunken snoring and the small, rhythmic puffs of her mother's breathing. She found the money he kept hidden in a tin box in the loft over the byre and took it without counting. Afterwards, on the boat to Holyhead, she found she had stolen seven hundred and sixty pounds.

She walked nine miles to catch the milk train to Dublin. The only sound the quick fall of her feet on deserted roads.

Not another living thing to break the silence.

Too early even for the blackbirds.

'Almost there now,' Gerry said as the car swept inexorably past the bridge and the flax-mill and down the remembered stretch of road to where the dark streel of mourners followed Father's coffin past the chapel gate. Through the open car window she could hear the murmur of voices and the muffled threat of the funeral bell, punching the air like an angry fist.

The mourners parted silently, absorbing her into their midst as she walked, bareheaded and heedless of the rain, between headstones etched with the familiar names that had once circumscribed her world. Brady, Mulligan, Maguire, Harten, Sheils, Reilly. From the townlands of Cornamucla, Corfree, Knockaughey, Salaghan, Dingins, Loughduff. Bastardisations of a dying language that tugged at the edges of her memory like the fragments of a half-remembered song.

She imagined the hurried judgements being made as slow voices dragging out the enormity of her crime. The passing of the decades since her going calculated by the events that marked their lives; deaths, elections, weddings, the year of the Big Wind.

'She must be gone out of the parish over thirty years.'

'Wouldn't you think that she'd have come home to wake her poor father?'

The words, flat as playing cards, slipping easily from the corners of knowing, half-smiling mouths as they tallied the sum of her neglect, with nods, winks, half-muffled smiles, as the news avidly spread that Chrissie was home from England in time to see poor John, her father, buried.

The rain was getting heavier, falling on the coffin lid like the irate drumming of impatient fingers. Someone moved to raise an umbrella over the priest and she caught the first glimpse of her mother, headscarved, dressed entirely in black, hovering uneasily at the edge of its shelter.

Gerry turned to her and touched her cheek with gentle fingers.

'All right, Mum?'

'All right love.'

She glanced gratefully at his thin, beautiful face and smiled back at him, comforted.

She took his arm and moved forward. The crowd shifted and gave way around her, averting their eyes from her as her father's coffin was lowered into the sodden earth. She was close enough now to see the dull gleam of brass handles, the raw, reddened hands of the men who held the broad, leather straps, the muscles of their necks roping against the strain. She felt as if she was looking down the wrong end of a telescope, the dutiful witness to the burial of a half-remembered stranger. She was almost irritated by the mediocrity of this moment that she had anticipated for years.

Gerry's arm was still around her, propelling her forward with gentle insistence to the place where her mother waited silently, a brown rosary snaking through her gloved fingers.

'You missed your father's Mass.'

The familiar voice was high-pitched and querulous as a child's.

'I suppose we should be thankful to God ye got here in time for the burial.'

Chrissie leaned forward and laid her cheek against the papery coldness of her mother's face, but the old woman pulled away and stepped back deferentially as the impatiently hovering priest reached forward and shook her hand with fingers that were slick with rain.

'So you got here.'

The words hung between them as he smiled with a smug folding of mottled lips and she realised that he was condemning her.

She was suddenly angry.

'It was unavoidable, Father, I was abroad when the news reached me.'

He ignored the remark, rocked back on his heels and examined her with narrowed eyes.

'You're very like your father, God rest his faithful soul. He was a fine man, poor John. A good Catholic and a devoted husband. Let you come up to the Parochial House for a chat before you leave us.'

The command in his voice was unmistakable.

She returned his smile coldly. *'Thank you, Father, I'll try.'*

She turned to her mother, ignoring the smothered outrage in the old woman's indrawn breath and the fury in the priest's eyes as he strode away with a curt little nod, hitching his cassock impatiently as he cut a respectful swarthe through the last of the gaping, slack-mouthed mourners.

'Hello, Mam, sorry we're late.'

She touched her mother's arm tentatively- shamed by the banality of her words.

'This is Gerry, your grandson.'

Her mother nodded stiffly, her eyes still angry.

'You were expected Friday. We waked your father for two days, waiting for you to come home.'

'I'm truly sorry, Mam, I was away when the news came. I got here as quickly as I could.'

But her mother had begun to pray, the singsong cadences an almost unintelligible murmur against the incessant sound of falling rain. *'Eternal rest Grant unto him, O Lord, and let perpetual light shine upon him.'* The beautiful words fell softly into the gathering darkness and the responses came back to Chrissie with an ease that startled her. *'May his soul, and the souls of all the faithful departed, rest in peace.'*

The undertaker tiptoed past them with exaggerated care and smiled placatingly as he placed two wreaths on the freshly turned earth, an ugly oval of blue, plastic roses from her mother and a defiant puddle of arum lilies and roses from Walter. A silver-etched dove watched with a knowing, beady eye from the corner of the card, just above her husband's name.

The brown soil humped sullenly over her father, raw and threatening in the gloom.

She had written twice. The first time to give her mother her address-the second, three years later, when she married Walter. She waited for a long time for a sign of either bitterness or rebuke, but none came. Father had seen to that.

The house was smaller, the lane narrower, than she remembered. Gerry finished his tea and stood up and stretched, smiling at them both.

'I'm going out for some air. It's been a long day.'

'Don't go too far.'

His eyes teased her.

'I know, don't talk to any strangers.'

The door closed softly behind him.

'He's a fine lad. A doctor, you tell me?' Her mother's voice was gentle.

'That's right.'

'It's a grand thing to have a doctor for a son. The lad has the look of your father.'

Chrissie crossed the room and touched her mother's stooped back.

'I'm sorry it took so long. But it was his fault I stayed away. He'd have sold me, his own daughter to Jamsie Soraghan for the sake of two sour fields.'

The words spewed from her, her voice thick with remembered rage.

Her mother carefully dried the good china cups that had belonged to her grandmother, polishing their rounded bellies on the corner of her apron.

'What odds now? Isn't it all in the past?' She said fiercely. *'Leave it be, can't you? Let the dead rest.'*

'Jamsie Soraghan was forty years older than me. He was an old man.'

She sat down again by the fire, holding her hands out to its warmth.

'I'm glad he's gone. Filthy, greedy old man. But I'll make up the lost time, Mam, I swear I'll make it up to you. When I think of all the years I've wasted in hating him. You never even had a chance to get to know Gerry, your own grandson.'

The slap was vicious, rocking her back in the chair as her mother leaned over her, white-faced with anger.

'You dirty trollop. What are you saying about the decent man that's not cold in his grave? You, that tumbled half-naked in the ditches with that whelp Halloran. And he running away and leaving you so that no decent boy would look at you or the side of the road you walked on.'

'The old woman groped blindly towards a chair and fell back, rocking herself back and forth, her eyes closed, her mouth working with grief and rage.

'Your poor father tried to cover your shame. He got you a good man that wouldn't scorn you and you paid him back his goodness by stealing all he owned in the world and running off in the dark of the night leaving two decent men to be the laughing stock of the country wide.'

'Mam.'

It was the high, bewildered wail of a child.

But her mother turned away and sat with bent head, her hands pleating and unpleating the flowered fabric of her apron as she prayed in a mumbled frantic monotone.

'Virgin of virgins, pray for us,
Mother most pure, pray for us,
Star of the sea, pray for us,
Queen of heaven pray for us.'

Chrissie opened the back door softly. The worn latch made a small, friendly cradle for her thumb.

The rain had stopped. The air was heavy with the perfume of woodbine and the sky, moon-washed, was the pale, translucent pearl of the inside of a shell. A drift of hawthorn soared triumphantly over the pigsty wall.

She sat quietly in the car with her hands folded in her lap.

Smiling to herself as she heard her son, Gerry, coming down the lane, whistling.